Three's
a Crowd

Cedar River Daydreams

1 • New Girl in Town
2 • Trouble with a Capital "T"
3 • Jennifer's Secret
4 • Journey to Nowhere
5 • Broken Promises
6 • The Intruder
7 • Silent Tears No More
8 • Fill My Empty Heart
9 • Yesterday's Dream
10 • Tomorrow's Promise
11 • Something Old, Something New
12 • Vanishing Star
13 • No Turning Back
14 • Second Chance
15 • Lost and Found
16 • Unheard Voices
17 • Lonely Girl
18 • More Than Friends
19 • Never Too Late
20 • The Discovery
21 • A Special Kind of Love
22 • Three's a Crowd
23 • Silent Thief
24 • The Suspect

9602

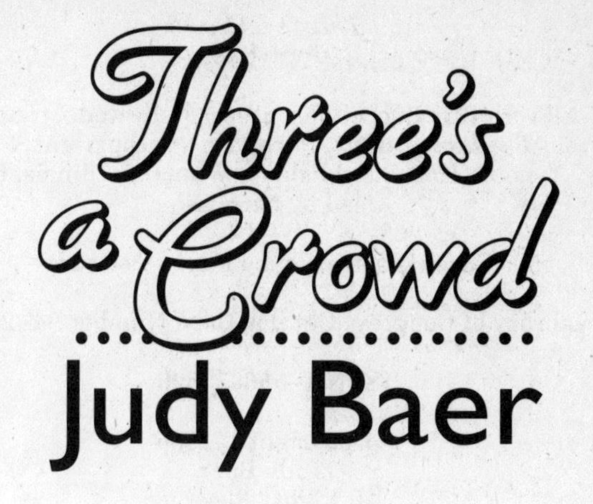

Judy Baer

BETHANY HOUSE PUBLISHERS
MINNEAPOLIS, MINNESOTA 55438

Three's a Crowd
Judy Baer

All scripture quotations, unless indicated, are taken from *The Living Bible, Paraphrased*, copyright © 1971, by Tyndale House Publishers, Wheaton, Illinois, 60187. Used by permission.

Cover illustration by Merry DeCourcy

Library of Congress Catalog Card Number 94–25133

ISBN 1–55661–526-4

Published by Bethany House Publishers
A Ministry of Bethany Fellowship, Inc.
11300 Hampshire Avenue South
Minneapolis, Minnesota 55438

Printed in the United States of America

For Jennifer and Katy,
who both “helped” me
write this book!

JUDY BAER received a B.A. in English and Education from Concordia College in Moorhead, Minnesota. She has had over thirty novels published and is a member of the National Romance Writers of America, the Society of Children's Book Writers, and the National Federation of Press Women.

Two of her novels, *Adrienne* and *Paige*, have been prizewinning bestsellers in the Bethany House SPRINGFLOWER SERIES (for girls 12–15). Both books have been awarded first place for juvenile fiction in the National Federation of Press Women's communications contest.

"Love is patient, love is kind. It does not envy, it does not boast, it is not proud. It is not rude, it is not self-seeking, it is not easily angered, it keeps no records of wrongs. Love does not delight in evil but rejoices with the truth. It always protects, always trusts, always hopes, always perseveres."

1 Corinthians 13:4–7

Chapter One

"You are on the verge of a new and exciting discovery. Life will take a definite turn for the better. Today you will meet a tall, dark, mysterious stranger who may change your life. Tonight is your night to party."

Binky McNaughton looked up from the horoscope section of the *Cedar River Daily* newspaper. "Do you think that means my brother Egg is going to move out of the house? I can't think of a better turn my life could take than that."

Lexi Leighton, Peggy Madison, and Jennifer Golden groaned in unison.

"Get over it, Binky," Jennifer commanded. "Are you still reading those stupid horoscopes? Haven't you figured out they're a complete piece of fiction?"

"Jennifer's right," Peggy agreed. "Someone is sitting in an office making up that garbage for people like you who actually read and believe it."

"I hope you aren't going to start looking for tall, dark strangers."

"Actually," Jennifer smirked, "a tall, dark encyclopedia salesman came to our house yesterday. He's canvassing Cedar River. He should be at your house soon."

"You're no fun." A pout formed at the corners of Binky's mouth. "And you're jealous because I have such a terrific horoscope today."

"Me? Jealous over tall, dark strangers? Ha!" Jennifer turned her nose in the air.

"A tall, dark, *mysterious* stranger," Binky amended. "And he's in *my* horoscope, while yours says that you'd better get to the bank because your checking account will be overdrawn."

"That much *is* true," Jennifer admitted. "Maybe there's something to this horoscope garbage after all."

"Binky, you aren't actually *serious* about this, are you?" Peggy looked bewildered.

"Kind of," Binky admitted. "I read my horoscope every day and something always comes true. How can that happen unless astrology really works?"

Lexi, who had been silent until now, cleared her throat. "That 'tall, dark, and handsome' stuff is a cliché, you know."

"Tall, dark, and *mysterious*," Binky corrected. "Besides, what harm can it do?"

"I suppose you have something there," Jennifer said. "It seems pretty harmless to read that little section of the newspaper every day."

"It may be harmless to read," Lexi interjected, "but it isn't harmless to believe it."

"You don't believe in this? Even just a little bit?" Binky ran her finger down the newspaper column. "Here's your horoscope for today, Lexi. Let's see what it says about you. . . . 'Beware of disagreements with your friends,' " Binky intoned. " 'Step back from trouble. Friendship is too valuable to waste. Tonight, get some exercise.' "

Binky looked up from the newspaper, her eyes sparkling triumphantly. "See? Your horoscope *predicted* that we would have a disagreement today. And we are—about horoscopes!"

"I'm inclined to agree with Lexi," Peggy commented. "I think horoscopes are a big scam. Somebody's got to be making money from them."

"They do seem kind of silly," Jennifer said, "but who's to say there isn't some truth in them? Astrology has been around a long time."

"I think it's real and true," Binky said. "I'm convinced that reading your horoscope can make a difference. I read mine every day. The days that it's bad, I'm very careful. Life is tough enough as it is. Who'd want to intentionally cross up their own horoscope?"

"Oh, Binky, you don't mean it." Lexi was dismayed. "You can't take that stuff seriously. . . ."

Binky dug deep into the pocket of her jeans and withdrew a small, dog-eared booklet. It was a cheap little paperback, the kind seen at checkout counters in grocery stores. The book's cover was navy blue and decorated with shapes of the sun, moon, and stars. Across it was a single word—*Horoscopes*.

"What's that?" Peggy eyed the little treatise suspiciously.

"My pocket horoscope, of course. It helps me keep track of what's going to happen each day, month, and year."

"Binky, you're not serious!"

Even Jennifer, who was less skeptical than the others, stared at Binky in dumbfounded amazement. "You mean you actually plan your *life* around that thing?"

"Not every second, silly." Binky looked hurt and indignant. "But I *am* cautious. I read my horoscope before I start any important project. I wouldn't want anything to go wrong."

"What kind of project?"

"Getting my hair permed, for example. Who needs a bad perm?"

Jennifer glared at her friend. "You're nuttier than I thought you were."

"Am not."

"Are too."

"Am not."

"Are too."

"Not."

"Too."

"Not."

"Too."

"Think about it, Bink. Horoscopes don't make sense. You were born in May. Right?"

"May twenty-seventh."

"That makes you a Gemini. Minda Hannaford's birthday is the first part of June. That also makes *her* a Gemini! Do you think you are anything like Minda Hannaford?" Peggy asked.

"Of course not. Don't even *say* it. I don't want to be compared in any way to that snooty, bossy, social-climbing . . ." Binky's voice trailed away as she began to realize what Peggy was getting at.

"That's *exactly* what I mean. You and Minda are nothing alike, yet you share the same horoscope. That means whatever is true for you is true for Minda too! Can you buy that?"

"You mean Minda is also going to meet a tall, dark, mysterious stranger today?"

"Exactly. Now your horoscope doesn't feel quite as special as it did before, does it?"

"You can't depend on a horoscope to plan your life," Lexi said softly.

"Besides," Jennifer added, "they *are* pretty generic."

"Most horoscopes could fit anyone on a certain day." Peggy grabbed the paper away from Binky. "Listen to this one—'Your friends will show great concern for you today. By early evening you will have realized the folly of your ways. Take it easy on yourself tonight.' Couldn't that horoscope apply to you as well?"

"I suppose," Binky admitted reluctantly.

"That was Scorpio's prediction. Now listen to this one." Peggy began to read again. " 'Family members will irritate you mightily today. Be patient. They can't help themselves.' "

Jennifer and Lexi began to hoot with laughter. "They must mean Egg!" The girls referred to Binky's strange but lovable older brother. He drove Binky crazy almost every day of her life.

"That's Aquarius's horoscope. Do you see what I mean, Binky? These things are interchangeable. You can't hang your hopes on a few sentences in a newspaper. You could read any of the horoscopes for today and find something that applied to you at this moment."

"You won't even try to understand, will you?" Binky complained.

"What is there to understand?"

"Astrology is a *science.*"

"Astrology is a *hoax.*"

Binky looked pityingly at her friends. "If it's

such a hoax, why do you see so many people wearing astrological signs? They're on jewelry, books, T-shirts, everything. How can reputable newspapers carry them if it's such a hoax? Can that many people be completely wrong?

"There *is* something to astrology," Binky continued. "I don't know exactly what it is yet, but there's got to be something there. Why risk ignoring your horoscope and having something go wrong? It doesn't make sense to take a chance."

One of Binky's outstanding characteristics was her stubbornness. When she got an idea into her head, she was as fierce as a little dog with a bone. She wouldn't let go of her idea until someone pried it loose. It was obvious that Lexi, Peggy, and Jennifer were not going to manage that now.

Peggy threw her hands into the air. "All right, believe that goofy stuff! Warp your mind! Act demented. See if we care."

Jennifer snapped her fingers. "I've got it! I know who the tall, dark, mysterious stranger is! Have any of you seen that new guy at school yet?"

Peggy's eyes grew dreamy. "Oh, *him*!"

Even Lexi had to smile. "His locker isn't far from mine. You're right, Jennifer. Tall, dark, and mysterious describes him perfectly."

Binky's freckle-spattered nose twitched with interest. "Really gorgeous, huh? What do you think my chances are that he'll come to the mall today and walk right by this table? I *am* destined to meet someone in the next few hours who fits his description."

"Big deal," Jennifer said with a shrug. "Every girl in Cedar River thinks she's destined to meet him in the next few hours. After phys ed the noise in the locker room was deafening because they were all so busy talking about him.

"He must pump iron. The first time I saw him he was wearing a T-shirt. He has the most *amazing* biceps." Jennifer flexed her much thinner arm in memory.

"He drives a little red convertible," Peggy added. "I saw it in the school parking lot."

"A convertible." Binky's eyes grew dreamy. "I've always wanted to date a guy with a convertible."

"Since when?" Jennifer asked in her usual blunt fashion. "The only guy you've ever dated is Harry Kramer, and I don't think Harry ever considered owning a convertible."

"A girl can dream, can't she?"

"I guess so," Jennifer conceded. "I hear he's really smart." A puckish grin flitted across her features. "I wonder if he'd be interested in tutoring someone who has severe dyslexia? Maybe Mister Tall, Dark, and Hunky could help me raise my grades."

"Like you'd get any studying done," Peggy retorted. "You'd be so busy staring into his eyes, you wouldn't know if you were looking at chemistry or accounting!"

"I don't anyway, so what's the difference?" Jennifer turned to Lexi. "What about you? What do you think?"

Lexi shrugged her shoulders lightly. "I don't know. He seems very nice. He asked me directions to one of his classes, so I walked him there. He told me his dad was just transferred to Cedar River. He said he'd wanted to stay behind and finish high school at his old school, but his parents insisted that he come with them. I told him that Cedar River was a pretty nice place to be and that I'd only moved here a year and a half ago myself."

"Oooh, things in common," Binky chirped. "A bond already!"

"Give it up, Binky," Lexi chided. "Walking someone to class does not make a relationship."

"A relationship. With who?" The girls turned to see Minda Hannaford and Gina Williams standing behind them holding submarine sandwiches.

"What are you talking about?" Gina demanded.

"That new guy at school," Peggy informed them.

"Oh, him." As if on cue, Minda and Gina plopped down beside the foursome.

"May we join you?" they asked after they were settled.

"Do we have a choice?" There was no lost love between Minda, Gina, and the other girls.

"Not really," Minda said, her mouth already full of her sandwich.

"All I know about him is that his name is Brock Taylor and he's an awesome hunk." Minda's blue eyes glittered. "And I'm going to find out more; I can promise you that."

"We don't doubt it for a minute," Jennifer assured her. "Brock might even *like* you . . . until he gets to *know* you."

Minda glared at Jennifer. "You're not funny, Golden."

"I didn't mean to be."

For the briefest moment Minda debated how to respond to Jennifer's jibe. Finally she shrugged good-naturedly, obviously having decided to ignore it.

"Anybody know anything else about him?"

"Red convertible, dad transferred, smart, hunky, weight lifter." Binky checked off the new boy's attributes on the tips of her fingers.

"Actually that's more than I'd heard before," Gina said. "No one at school seems to know much about him."

"Aha," Binky crowed in triumph. "And he's *mysterious* too!"

"Huh?" Minda and Gina stared at Binky in bewilderment. Peggy, Lexi, and Jennifer groaned.

"My horoscope is right after all! It said I was going to meet a tall, dark, mysterious stranger today."

"But you haven't met him," Lexi pointed out gently. "All you've done is listen to us talk about him."

"Same thing," Binky said with a wave of her hand. "He came into my life today. On the day my horoscope said it would happen. Don't you think that's absolutely fascinating? It's proof positive that my horoscope was correct. These things really work. I *told* you so!"

"Isn't there anything else we can talk about," Lexi asked desperately. "You know I don't believe in horoscopes, and all this talk about the new guy is boring."

"Boring to *you* maybe," Gina pointed out, "but that's because you already have a boyfriend. Why would you want to think about anyone else when you have Todd Winston?"

Todd had been Lexi's close friend since she moved to Cedar River. There was truth in Gina's words. Why *would* any girl want to look at another guy when she had Todd Winston in her life? He was one of the most attractive, considerate boys in Cedar River. Lexi knew she was fortunate to have him as her friend.

"I'm done eating. How about you?" Gina corralled a piece of stray lettuce and popped it into her mouth. "Ready to go?"

"Anytime." Minda crumpled the paper in which her sandwich had been wrapped and stuffed it into her beverage glass. "It has been super talking to you girls," she said insincerely, "but we have got to go now."

"Don't let us hold you up," Jennifer growled. After they had departed, she rolled her eyes and groaned. "Those two drive me nuts!"

"Give them a break," Lexi commented. "Last year Minda wouldn't have sat down and talked with us at all. I think she's improving."

"If she *is*, it's not happening fast enough for me. She's still conceited, egotistical, selfish, pampered, spoiled rotten . . ."

"Let's not ruin this day by talking about Minda," Binky pleaded. "I want to talk some more about Tall, Dark, and Mysterious."

"Would you settle for tall, skinny, and goofy looking?" Jennifer's gaze was directed over Binky's shoulder. Binky turned around to see her brother, Egg, ambling toward them, with Todd Winston at his side.

Todd was dressed in faded jeans and a white shirt. His blond hair feathered away from his face except for an errant lock that tumbled rebelliously over his eye.

Egg McNaughton walked jerkily beside him. Egg's distinctive rambling gait was even more pronounced because he was limping.

"What happened to you?"

Egg thrust out a foot to reveal a pair of new shoes. "I'm trying to break them in, but all I've done so far is get a blister."

"You're at the mall breaking in a pair of shoes?"

"Can you think of a better place to walk?" Egg plopped into a chair and began to rub his heel. "They must build razor blades into shoes nowadays. My feet are killing me."

"Let's go back to the car and get your tennis shoes," Todd suggested.

"Not yet. These shoes aren't completely broken in."

"What good will they do if you can't walk?"

"How did he talk you into coming out here?" Binky asked Todd.

"He bribed me with food. He said he'd buy me a milk shake if I hung in with him two laps around the mall."

"You got the bad end of that deal."

Todd's even white teeth flashed as he grinned. "You forget how entertaining your brother is."

Binky snorted. "Personally, I find everything he does humiliating."

By this time Egg had removed his shoe and sock and was massaging his sore heel with an ice cube from the water glass on the table.

"See what I mean?" Binky pointed at Egg's toes. "Totally humiliating."

Everyone laughed. They were so accustomed to

Egg and his curious ways that nothing he did surprised them anymore.

Lexi caught Todd's wink. "Are you going to be home by seven?" she asked softly.

"Do you two have a date tonight?" Egg inquired. "Why didn't you say so? I could have broken these shoes in tomorrow."

"It's okay," Todd said. "We don't have anything formal planned."

"Be sure to come by early. My little brother Ben has a surprise for you."

"I already know what it is." Todd's blue eyes twinkled. "I talked to your dad yesterday."

"What kind of surprise?" Binky asked. "Something I'd like?"

Lexi burst out laughing. "Actually, it is. My dad brought Ben a puppy."

"Oooh, a puppy," Binky cooed. "I love puppies. What kind is it?"

"A mixed breed. Someone brought it into Dad's veterinary clinic and said they didn't want it anymore. The puppy was so sweet that Dad decided to bring it home for Ben. After all, Benjamin has been campaigning for a dog for a long time.

"Dad thinks Ben and this puppy will be great buddies. Ben is so anxious to show him to you, Todd, that it took both Mom and Dad to convince him that he shouldn't call you at five this morning to have you come over and see his new pet."

"Why five o'clock?" Peg asked.

"That's when the puppy got us all out of bed. It's worse than having a baby in the house!"

"What's the dog's name?"

"Wiggles. That tells you something about this puppy, doesn't it?"

Todd glanced at his watch and then poked at Egg with the toe of his boot. "Come on, Egg. If you're going to hobble around this mall one more time before supper, we'd better hurry. I don't want to be late for my date and miss the opportunity to meet Wiggles!"

Chapter Two

The Leightons' doorbell rang promptly at seven. A scramble of squeals and footsteps preceded Lexi as she headed for the door to greet Todd.

Immediately Ben and his small, fat puppy barreled into him. Ben's silky dark hair was full of static electricity and flew wildly around his chubby face. His dark, almond-shaped eyes, so characteristic of a Down's syndrome child, sparkled gleefully. A furry, wiggly mass of brown and white somersaulted over its own tail to land at Todd's feet. The puppy immediately began to chew on the lace of Todd's sneaker.

"This is my new puppy, Todd. Isn't he beeyu—tiful?"

Todd scrunched down to scratch behind the puppy's ears. The puppy began to lick Todd's fingers. "Hi there, little guy," Todd crooned to the pup. "Aren't you a handsome fellow? What's your name?"

"His name is Wiggles," Ben chortled.

In response to his name, the puppy gave a squirmy shudder. His pencil-thin tail pounded softly on the floor.

"He doesn't look like a Wiggles," Todd teased as

the puppy squirmed and writhed.

"Yes he does. Look at him. He's wiggling right now." Ben jumped up and down on his tiptoes. "I named him myself, didn't I, Lexi?"

Lexi, who had been watching the activity from the sidelines, nodded and laughed. "It was between Wiggles and Chewy. And you can tell why either name would be appropriate." She pointed to Todd's shoelace. Wiggles had already gnawed it nearly in half.

"No, no, puppy mustn't chew." Ben dropped first to all fours and then to his stomach beside the dog. The puppy, seeing his master so close by, gave a delighted little yip and rolled to its feet. It toddled to where Ben lay and began to lick the boy's face. Delighted laughter erupted from Ben. Soon a chorus of giggling and playful growling emanated from the pair on the floor.

"Ben's wanted a puppy practically forever," Lexi commented. "When Dad saw this one come in, unwanted, he just couldn't take it to the Humane Society. He had to bring it home for Ben."

"What's the hoo-maine society?" Ben asked.

"That's where people can take animals who don't have homes," Lexi explained. "It's an organization that makes sure that our animals are treated kindly. If an animal is lost or is a stray, the Humane Society will try to find homes for them."

"Then let's go to the hoo-maine society and get some more pets," Ben suggested. "Wiggles needs a playmate."

"It looks to me as though he has one." Todd pointed a finger at Ben's nose. "You."

"Next I want a kitty, then another rabbit and

then . . ." Ben looked up with inquiring eyes. "Do they have ponies at the hoo-maine society?"

"I think you'd better learn how to take care of Wiggles first," Lexi suggested mildly. "You have to learn how to feed him, to walk him, and to groom him."

"What's groom?"

"Comb his hair."

"With my hairbrush?"

"No, we'll get Wiggles his own brush."

Todd cleared his throat. "I thought of another name for your puppy that might even be more appropriate. Puddles."

Lexi's eyes widened. She looked down at the spreading stain leaking around Wiggles and onto the carpet.

"Oh, oh," Ben said. "Time to walk the puppy." Ben shot for the door. Lexi's and Todd's laughter followed him.

"Isn't that a little like closing the barn door after the horse has already escaped?" Todd smothered a chuckle.

Lexi stared ruefully at the stain on the carpet. "Are you in a big hurry or can you wait a minute until I clean up this mess?"

"You're a soft touch for a sister," Todd said with a laugh. "I thought you'd make poor little Ben and Wiggles clean it up."

"Maybe tomorrow. They're both so excited right now that I think it's a hopeless cause."

While Lexi tended to her housekeeping chore, Todd sat at the kitchen counter leafing through a magazine. When Lexi returned to the kitchen he opened to an article he'd found. "Here's a story on the Humane Society. You'll have to show it to Ben."

"I really am glad Dad brought Wiggles home. It breaks my heart to think of animals left homeless or abandoned because humans are careless." Before Lexi could say more, Ben and Wiggles came roaring into the kitchen. Wiggles's fat little belly swung from side to side as he ran.

"I'm going to bed," Ben announced.

Lexi's eyes grew wide with surprise. "Now? It's not your bedtime yet."

Ben scooped the puppy into his arms. "I'm going to bed and Wiggles is going to sleep with me." He touched his nose to the cold, wet one. "Isn't that right, Wiggles?"

Lexi rolled her eyes and grabbed Todd's hand. "Let's get out of here before I have to hear my mother's opinion on this idea." Lexi and Todd escaped through the front door while Ben, with Wiggles under one arm, trudged upstairs to the bedroom.

Todd was uncharacteristically quiet while they bowled. Over fries and milk shakes he sank into silence, making Lexi feel uncomfortable. "You're very quiet tonight. Does anything special account for this strange mood you're in?"

Todd stirred thoughtfully at his milk shake with the tip of his straw. "Sorry."

"It's not a crime, you know," Lexi attempted to joke. "Is there something wrong?"

"No," Todd shook his head. "Nothing's wrong."

"What is it, then?"

"I have something I want to say and I'm having a hard time getting it out."

"You can say anything to me, Todd. You should know that by now." Lexi had never seen Todd like this before. What was wrong?

In the dim light his eyes took on the hue of violets. Somehow, Lexi felt as though Todd could see right through her.

"You and I have been friends for a long time, haven't we?"

"Ever since my family moved to Cedar River. I'll never forget how surprised I was to learn that you knew my little brother Ben even before you and I met. I was worried that you wouldn't be able to accept my handicapped brother—and you'd already become his best buddy.

"One of the nicest things that ever happened to me, Todd, was realizing that you knew about Ben and loved him for himself."

Not everyone was comfortable around handicapped children. Lexi had learned that the hard way. It had been a real gift to find someone like Todd who understood Ben's limitations and accepted him just as he was.

"Have you dated any other guys since we met?" Todd asked.

"I've gone places with guys," Lexi admitted, "but always in groups. You know that. You're usually in the group too."

What was making Todd act so odd?

Todd took Lexi's hand in his own.

"We've been together for a long time now. I was just wondering . . . I'd like it if . . . we could . . . is it possible that . . . you'd be willing to go steady?"

Lexi smiled. "As far as I can tell, we *already* are! Neither of us dates anyone else."

Some of the tension melted from Todd's features. "Remember when we ordered our class rings?"

Lexi hadn't purchased a ring. Instead she'd ordered a little gold pendant embossed with the year of her graduation.

"My ring will be coming soon," Todd continued, "and I was wondering if you'd be willing to wear it."

"Todd, I . . ." Lexi was stunned. The thought of *officially* going steady had never entered her mind. "Are you trying to give your ring away before you even get an opportunity to wear it for yourself?"

"I might wear it a week or two, but after that . . ." Todd paused, letting Lexi finish the sentence for herself.

"I don't know," she stammered. "You really caught me off guard."

"This is something I've been thinking about for a long time. It would make me very happy if you'd wear my ring. I want to show others how much we mean to each other."

Lexi felt suffused with a warm glow. "This is one of the nicest things that's ever happened to me. Thank you."

"You're welcome. But does that mean yes or no?"

"What about my parents? Mom and Dad aren't big on teenagers tying themselves down as couples. I'm not sure they'll approve." Lexi wasn't even quite sure that *she* approved! "And what about all the talks we've had about being such good friends?"

"That will never change with us, Lexi. We'll always be friends. The only difference is that now you'll have my ring." Todd's warm gaze roamed across her face.

Lexi's throat grew dry and her heart pounded.

"This is serious, Todd."

"It's just making official everything we've always felt for each other," he said matter-of-factly. "I want everyone to know you're my girl."

"I need time to think. . . . I have to consider what my parents might say. Could I have a little time?"

The corners of Todd's mouth tipped upward in a smile. "Take all the time you need, Lexi. Just so you come up with the right answer."

Lexi flip-flopped restlessly in her bed. Her sheets and blanket were tangled around her ankles in a wadded ball. To untangle her feet, Lexi swung her legs over the side of the bed and stood up. She padded softly to the window.

Her father had been up thirty minutes ago with Wiggles.

Ben, who had enthusiastically promised to take the puppy outside at night, had fallen promptly and soundly asleep, oblivious to the puppy's persistent whining.

Lexi stared out at the streetlights as they cast ghostly shadows on the lawn.

"What do I *do*?" Lexi felt torn apart inside. She wanted desperately to be Todd's exclusive girlfriend. It was wonderful to know how deeply he felt about her. What's more, she'd never met another boy she liked as well as she liked Todd. He was kind, considerate, thoughtful, funny, generous, sweet, handsome . . . everything she could ever want in a boyfriend.

Still, she knew that her parents would feel more

comfortable if they'd each had more opportunities to date others.

Lexi sighed and leaned her forehead against the cool pane of window glass. Maybe she was blowing things out of proportion.

After all, Todd hadn't asked her to marry him, just to be his girlfriend. In reality she was *already* Todd's steady. So why did it scare her to think of making it official?

Chapter Three

Lexi hurried down the school corridor with Binky beside her. Binky had her nose buried in a small paperback book. Every few moments she'd blurt out another tidbit of astrological information.

"Listen to this—'Your employer will be cranky today, but do not despair. Good news is to be had later.' " Binky looked up from her book of horoscopes with a hopeful expression. "Do you think 'employer' could also mean 'teacher'? Teachers are *our* bosses after all, especially if we don't have another job. Every teacher is cranky today. I wonder if that means I'm going to be getting *A*'s in all my classes? Wouldn't that be great?"

"The only way to get *A*'s in your classes, Binky, is to do your homework and study for tests." Lexi was getting tired of horoscopes, *very tired.*

Binky wrinkled her nose at that suggestion. A horoscope prediction was more appealing and much less work.

Her attention span, short in the best of times, was absolutely minuscule today. "Do you know anyone who is an Aries, Lexi? Aries' horoscope says that today is a great day to be 'bold and forceful.'

That would be a good bit of information to have, don't you think?"

"Oh, Binky, you know I don't believe in that stuff. Why do you keep tormenting me with it?"

"Lighten up, Lexi. I'm just having some fun . . ." Binky's voice trailed away as she buried her nose in the book again.

Uninterested in Binky's horoscopes, Lexi glanced toward the nearest exit. Coming down the hall toward them was a tall, well-built young man with dark hair and the most incredible eyes she'd ever seen. They weren't blue and they weren't green. They were—was it possible?—turquoise.

The attractive young man sauntered toward them with athletic grace. A dark forelock drifted lazily over one eye. His hair was cut short in front but was long in the back and gathered neatly into a short ponytail.

"Binky, wake up." Lexi jabbed at her friend with her elbow.

"Huh!" Binky looked up owlishly from the page. She blinked once or twice before focusing on the young man approaching them.

"It's Tall, Dark, and Mysterious. It's no surprise everybody's talking about Brock Taylor. Cute, isn't he?"

"Cute?" Binky echoed. "Brock Taylor is gorgeous."

She narrowed her eyes and studied him. "I wonder if he's a Capricorn. My birth sign is compatible with Capricorns. . . ."

As they met in the center of the hallway, Brock greeted the girls with a dazzling smile, perfect except for a tiny overlap of one front tooth that somehow managed to make him appear even more appealing.

"Hi there."

"Hi, yourself." Butterflies began to flutter against Lexi's rib cage.

"Can you tell me where the school counselor's office is? I'm supposed to stop there to answer some questions about my file."

Binky gaped at the boy as though she didn't even know that Cedar River High School had a school counselor.

"Hang a left at the end of this hall," Lexi said. "Three doors past the lunchroom."

"Great, thanks a lot." He magnified the wattage of his smile. "My name's Brock Taylor. I think we've met before but I've forgotten your name."

"L . . . L . . . Lexi." She actually felt tongue-tied. "And this is my friend Binky," she added as an afterthought.

Brock was about to speak when Tressa and Gina Williams burst out of a nearby classroom.

The sisters exchanged predatory glances and turned in Brock's direction.

"Here you are again," Gina purred. "Did you get all your classes straightened out?"

Brock gave her the same wide smile he'd just bestowed on Lexi and Binky. "Almost. I should have everything squared away by tomorrow. It's not easy transferring schools."

"I'm sure it's not," Tressa empathized. "But if there's anything we can do to help . . ."

". . . anything at all . . ."

". . . just let us know."

Binky made a gagging sound as the sisters blatantly threw themselves at Brock, flirting and giggling shamelessly.

"Where are you going right now?" Gina asked.

"I was getting directions to the school counselor's office. I need to get down there before . . ."

"We'll take you!" Tressa looped her hand through the crook of Brock's arm and started down the hall with him.

"Hey, wait for me," Gina complained as she latched possessively on to his other arm.

As the two girls drew him away, Brock looked back at Lexi and shrugged his shoulders helplessly.

"Give me a break," Binky growled. "Have you ever seen women chase a man like that?"

"He went with them, didn't he?" Lexi said with a smile.

"Yes, and willingly too. But what was that look about?"

"What look?" Lexi asked mildly.

"That look he gave you as they pulled him away. It was as though you had this . . . connection."

"Oh, come off it, Binky. You've been reading too many love stories. Eyeballs can't connect. We should be grateful for it too. Otherwise we'd have a terrible mess of eyeballs tangled up on the floor in the hallway . . ."

"Don't try to joke your way out of this, Lexi. I saw how he looked at you. And I saw how *you* looked at him."

"And how was that?" Lexi felt a blush bleed across her cheeks.

"Steamy, that's how. Brock gave you a pretty steamy look for just having met you."

Lexi couldn't deny what Binky had said. She

had felt the connection between herself and Brock and wasn't quite sure what to make of it. The only other time she'd felt this way was when she'd met Todd Winston.

"What are you thinking? Why are you so quiet?" Binky had stowed her horoscope and was peering at Lexi with unabashed interest.

"I was just thinking that you're right, Binky. Brock Taylor *is* a good-looking guy."

The music room was in chaos when Lexi and Jennifer entered. The music stands were a tangled mass and no one could find the music that Mrs. Waverly had requested.

Egg and Todd were moving a piano across the room. Everyone else appeared completely unfocused. Everyone except, that is, Minda Hannaford. She was utterly focused—on Brock Taylor.

"The sharks are out today," Jennifer commented casually. "Must be fresh blood in the water."

"Quiet, Jennifer. Someone might hear you," Lexi cautioned.

"I don't care. Everyone knows how Minda behaves when there's a new guy in school. She wants him all to herself." Jennifer paused. "Frankly, this time I can't blame her. I'd like a hunk like that for myself too."

"I think you're too late." Binky inclined her head toward the back of the room where Brock and Minda were talking. "If Minda bats her eyelashes any faster, she's going to propel herself right into the air."

Lexi put a hand over her mouth to hide a giggle.

It was true. Minda was flirting so obviously that it was laughable. She talked expansively with her hands, brushing the tip of one finger against Brock's cheek.

"Who does Minda think she is? Hitting on him like that?" Jennifer growled.

"What else do you expect from her?" Binky asked. "He *is* gorgeous, in case you've forgotten."

"She should be ashamed of herself." Jennifer peered at the pair. "Do you think he's falling for it? Her coy little flirtation, I mean. I hope he's smart enough to see through her."

"Time will tell." Lexi resolutely put the image of Brock and Minda out of her mind. She turned toward Todd and gave him her brightest smile.

As long as Minda was interested in Brock she would leave Todd alone. There was always good news in every situation, Lexi decided, though sometimes it meant looking hard to find it.

"Put your music in the proper order in file folders, please. And, Lexi," Mrs. Waverly added, "you're missing two pieces of music which I borrowed from your folder. Please pick them up before you leave the room."

Everyone had filed out by the time Lexi had retrieved her music and put it away. She was surprised to find Brock waiting for her by the music room door.

"What are you doing out here?"

"I wanted to talk to you."

Lexi looked around for signs of Minda. She thought she saw a flutter of royal blue turn the corner at the end of the hallway. Minda had probably been waiting, hoping to waylay Brock there.

"Mrs. Waverly suggested I talk to you about joining the Emerald Tones." Brock referred to the musical group to which Lexi belonged. "She told me you could give me the details on tryouts and practice times. I belonged to a band back east. I was the drummer, but I enjoy singing. I don't want to get involved with another band. It takes too much time. The Emerald Tones sounds like a good alternative."

"Then you've come to the right person. I love being a member of the Emerald Tones. There is so much to tell you I hardly know where to start. . . ."

They were still talking when they reached their lockers.

Binky and Peggy were waiting there. Binky shifted her weight impatiently from one foot to the other and Peggy clutched her school books close to her chest.

"Sorry I took so much of your time," Brock said. "Thanks for the information." He turned on the ball of his foot and started down the hall before Lexi could say more.

"I didn't mean to keep you waiting," Lexi apologized. "Is anything wrong. . . ." Her voice trailed away as she saw the grimace on Binky's face.

Lexi turned around to see Minda bearing down on her, cheeks red and eyes bright with fury.

"All right, Leighton, what's the idea?" Minda anchored her hands on her hips and glared at Lexi menacingly. Lexi couldn't ever remember seeing her look quite so furious.

"What are you talking about?"

"All that blatant flirting with Brock? What's the idea?"

"Flirting?" Lexi was dumbfounded. "We were

talking about the Emerald Tones! Mrs. Waverly told him he should ask me some questions about joining the group."

"Right. Little Miss Innocent. You were smiling at him too sweetly just to be talking about music."

"Is that so awful? I didn't see a 'Do Not Talk to the New Boy in School' sign around Brock's neck. We were just talking. It was no big deal."

"Minda didn't want you to steal the new boy away from her," Binky chimed. "You know how *possessive* Minda is about new guys at school."

"Stay out of this, McNaughton."

"Why? You're bent out of shape because Brock flirted with Lexi instead of with you."

"Binky!" Lexi's tone stopped Binky in midsentence.

"Well, that's how it looked to me," Binky grumbled.

"You guys are hopeless, just hopeless." Minda spun around and stomped off, her head held high.

Peggy made a clucking sound at the back of her throat. "My, my, wasn't that interesting? She must really have the hots for this new guy. Even Minda isn't usually *that* possessive."

"Can you blame her? He's cute."

"I don't want to hear any more about Minda or Brock." Lexi looked at the pair across from her. "You weren't waiting here just to hear that little exchange between Minda and me, were you?"

"We're getting together for pizza at my house tonight. Anna Marie is coming and she hasn't been with us for ages. Can you make it?"

"I'll be there." At least Lexi wouldn't run into Minda at Peggy's.

"Why don't we do this more often?" Anna Marie Arnold wondered as she chased a string of mozzarella cheese that was dangling from her slice of pizza.

"Let's make a plan," Binky suggested, hanging her feet over the edge of Peggy's bed. "Once a month, pizza at somebody's house. We'll take turns. We can do it at my place next. Egg can cook."

"Is that supposed to make us *want* to come?" Jennifer inquired. "We know how Egg is in the kitchen."

"He makes a pretty mean pizza," Binky said graciously. "It's just that he's an idiot at everything else."

"Don't be so hard on Egg," Anna Marie said. "He's very sweet."

"Are you talking about *my* brother?" Binky shuddered.

"By the way, where is Egg tonight?"

"I made him go to Todd's. He and Matt are watching the ball game."

"So it's guys' night out too," Anna Marie deduced. "Speaking of guys, what does everyone think of the new guy in school?"

"Let's not talk about Brock again," Lexi pleaded. "Minda Hannaford is after him. She almost bit my head off for talking to him after choir today."

"Minda's going to have competition." Anna Marie plucked a pepperoni slice off the top of the pizza and popped it into her mouth. "I have three classes with him and the girls are all absolutely goofy about him. Beth Jones was so busy looking at him that she tripped on a garbage can in math class and ended up sprawled across his desk. You should have seen the look on Brock's face!"

"He isn't much affected by the attention," Peggy observed. "I think I like him. He's not stuck up."

"He's probably used to girls falling at his feet."

"Anybody that good-looking would have to be popular."

"I'm not sure he even knows he's good-looking," Lexi commented. "He seems like a nice guy."

"I've heard that he's moved a lot because of his parents." Peggy opened another liter of cola. "His dad's been in the military. Brock's traveled all over the world."

"Handsome and world traveler too! Can you believe that? It just gets better and better."

"Isn't there *anything* else to talk about?" Lexi asked, exasperated.

"You usually don't mind talking about boys, Lexi," Jennifer teased. "What makes Brock so different? Is it the fact that Brock seems exceptionally friendly toward you?"

Lexi brushed off Jennifer's statement with a flick of her hand. "He's nice to everyone. You said that yourself."

"But he's *especially* nice to you," Binky took up Jennifer's refrain.

Lexi felt a blush stain her cheeks. It made her uncomfortable to be the brunt of all this attention. "It's no big deal. I wish you'd quit trying to make it into one."

Binky made a dive for her backpack and pulled out the tattered horoscope book she carried. "I'm going to see what your horoscope says for this month!" She leafed through the pages.

"Ah, here it is. 'Remain upbeat,' " she intoned. " 'Someone new and special will enter your life shortly. Listen to your heart, but beware of a bad decision that could hurt you forever.' "

Binky looked up from the book, her eyes large. "Oooh, scary!"

"What's scary about that?"

"Don't you see? It's telling you about Brock!"

"I didn't hear his name mentioned, Binky."

Binky gave her a look of disgust.

"It's all right here—if you'd only believe it. Something is going to happen with Brock, and I think Todd will be involved as well." Binky wore her best fortune-teller expression.

"Get real, Binky," Lexi pleaded. The entire conversation made her very uncomfortable.

But Binky was not about to be sidetracked.

"You may not believe me yet, Lexi, but I have *proof* that horoscopes come true! Last week, my mom's said, 'Be careful with your funds. Do not rush into hasty investments. But remember, money isn't everything.' "

"That's proof?"

"She kept thinking about that warning all day. Finally Mom decided to balance her checkbook, and do you know what? *She was overdrawn!* If it hadn't been for that horoscope, she would have received a finance charge from the bank!"

"Binky . . ."

"And there's more. Two days ago I read my dad his horoscope. It said, 'Don't be so negative. Things are not as bad as they seem. Remain cheerful. Your superiors know best.' "

Binky paused dramatically. "And that afternoon, Dad got a raise! Isn't that wonderful?"

"I'm very happy for your father, but I don't think the horoscope had anything to do with it."

"How can you doubt? Especially when all of these things come true?"

"Those horoscopes are so general that they could apply to anyone," Lexi protested.

"What's wrong with you today, Lexi?" Binky blurted.

"I can't help it, Binky. I'm *uncomfortable* with horoscopes."

"How can this make you uncomfortable? Even my dad calls it 'harmless fun.' "

"It just doesn't jive with what I know about God, that's all. If I want guidance in my life, I turn to Him, not convenient phrases in a newspaper or a magazine. It's *wrong*—sinful—to believe that the stars can determine your life for you."

Binky's mouth puckered. "I never thought about it quite like that. I wouldn't want to be doing anything that went against God's commandments. Are you sure about this, Lexi? I don't want to do anything wrong. . . ." Binky chewed thoughtfully on her lower lip. "I wonder if there's any way for me to get the real scoop on horoscopes."

Lexi didn't answer. She was trying hard to give full attention to her friend. Though she wouldn't have admitted it to anyone, she was still thinking about Brock Taylor.

Chapter Four

"Is there more popcorn?" Binky's head hung over the side of Lexi's bed Friday night. Her comical little face looked even funnier when viewed upside down.

"Don't tell me you've eaten it already."

Jennifer snaked out a foot and kicked a plastic bowl of popcorn into Binky's line of vision. "Here. Help yourself."

Binky flipped from her back to her stomach and buried both hands up to her knobby wrists in popcorn.

"Who wants to read the next poem?" Peggy inquired. "It's Robert Frost."

"I'll do it," Lexi volunteered.

"I study so much better at slumber parties, don't you?" Binky filled her mouth with popcorn until her cheeks stuck out like those of a squirrel hoarding nuts.

"How can you eat so much and stay so little?" Jennifer asked.

"You haven't quit eating since we got here."

"It's true, Binky, you've either been chewing or talking for the last four hours."

"Isn't it great?" Binky gave a blissful shudder.

"I'm celebrating being away from Egg. My brother's been such a pain in the neck lately. I borrowed one of his shirts for school yesterday and he had a fit because I spilled a little spaghetti sauce on it."

"It wasn't just a *little* spaghetti sauce," Peggy reminded her. "I saw you dump your entire plate down the front of that shirt."

"It was an accident. Besides, it was Egg who shaved the hair off all my dolls' heads when I was in the second grade. That was a *deliberate* act. The spaghetti was *accidental*."

"What are the guys doing tonight?" Lexi asked.

"Egg and Jerry are meeting Todd over at Mike's garage. They're all planning to work on Matt Windsor's motorcycle."

"Todd spends a lot of time at his brother's garage now, doesn't he?"

The boys had been going to Mike's shop more often since the death of Mike's fiancee, Nancy. It was their way of showing support for Mike and keeping him company as well. Nancy had been a friend to many of the kids in Cedar River. They all missed her a great deal.

"Todd likes to be around just in case his brother needs him. Mike's assistant, Ed Bell, is on vacation right now, but as soon as he comes back to work, Todd will have more free time." Lexi grinned impishly. "I can hardly wait."

"You and Todd have a unique relationship, don't you?" Peggy commented enviously.

Lexi looked up from her notebook. "What do you mean?"

"You and Todd are *friends* as well as being boyfriend and girlfriend. When I dated Chad it wasn't like that at all." Peggy's features darkened. Chad had fathered the baby Peggy had given up for adoption. Later he had committed suicide. Peggy rarely mentioned his name.

"Chad and I were boyfriend and girlfriend, but we were never best friends. It's not like that for you at all, is it?"

"Todd and I are lucky—we really *are* best friends."

Jennifer gave an unladylike snort. "That's what you *always* say. 'We're best friends.' Admit it, Lexi, you and Todd are *crazy* about each other."

Lexi blushed. "You know what my mom and dad say about going steady in high school. They don't think it's a good idea."

"Maybe, but that 'just best friends' line is getting old. Unless you start dating some other guys, no one is going to believe your story."

"Guys like Brock," Binky offered helpfully. "Cute and nice too."

"Can't you girls think of anything but—" A commotion erupted outside Lexi's room.

Ben barreled into the room squealing at the top of his lungs. Alongside him toddled a yapping puppy.

Binky knelt down on the floor beside the boy and his dog. "He's darling, Ben!"

Before Ben could respond, the puppy demonstrated the reason for his name, wagging his tail until his whole body shuddered with glee. Ben sat down on the floor and picked up the puppy. Wiggles promptly began to lick the underside of Ben's chin. The harder the puppy licked, the more Ben giggled.

"Isn't that cute?" Binky watched the pair with undisguised delight.

"Cuter than what the puppy was doing earlier." Lexi held up a tennis shoe filled with tiny teeth marks. "I bought these shoes last week and now look at them."

"How can you resist? . . . What's he doing now?"

Wiggles tumbled away from Ben and dashed headlong across the room as fast as his chubby little legs would take him. The puppy almost careened into the wall before turning to dash in the opposite direction.

"My dad calls that 'frenetic puppy activity.' He's not sure why puppies do it, but every once in a while they simply like to race around at breakneck speeds."

"I think it's adorable," Jennifer said.

Ben squealed and clapped his hands with delight.

Lexi eyed Wiggles suspiciously as the pup sniffed frantically around the leg of her desk chair. "Ben, when was the last time you took the puppy outside?"

"I don't remember."

"Benjamin, you know what Dad told you about taking the puppy out . . ." Lexi's warning came too late. A puddle began to spread across the carpet.

"Not here, Wiggles!" Ben squealed.

"Now what?" Jennifer looked down at the puddle on the floor.

"Spot remover and paper towels," Lexi said with a sigh. "That puppy is going to give me gray hair. Excuse me while I get the stuff to clean up this mess. Benjamin, take the puppy out . . . now!"

The last they saw of the two was Wiggles's little tail wagging and the heels of Ben's shoes.

When the phone rang, Jennifer was the first to reach it. "Hello, Leighton residence."

"Lexi, it's for you," Jennifer hissed. "It's a guy."

"Todd?"

"I don't think so."

"Jerry? Matt?" Lexi ticked off the names of the boys who were likely to call her.

"It doesn't sound like any of them." Jennifer thrust the receiver into Lexi's hand. "Find out for yourself."

Binky, Jennifer, and Peggy leaned forward to listen.

"Oh, hi, Brock. How are you?"

"Brock!" Binky whispered. "What's *he* calling for?"

Lexi wondered the same thing. The conversation meandered from one topic to another for several minutes before Brock arrived at the point of his call.

"I have a really big favor to ask of you," he admitted.

"Name it." Lexi's curiosity was growing by leaps and bounds.

"Since we share several classes, would you be willing to help me with some homework assignments? I'm behind because of our move. It won't take much for me to catch up, but I do need to borrow class notes and have someone tell me what material has been covered. I was just wondering if you . . ." His voice trailed away.

Lexi was shocked into silence.

"I know you're on the honor roll. My teachers

suggested some names to me and yours was one of them. If you'd rather not do it, I'll understand."

"I . . . uh . . . well . . ."

"Feel free to tell me to bug off. I don't want to be any trouble."

"No trouble," Lexi finally managed. "It shouldn't take very long. Just a few evenings to cover what's been taught."

"Then you'll do it? I was hoping you'd say yes. It will be a chance for me to get to know you. I'll call you tomorrow night to set up a time to get started."

Lexi could hear the delight in Brock's voice and she nodded dumbly into the telephone. Brock didn't seem to mind her silence.

"Thanks a lot, Lexi. I'm looking forward to this. Talk to you tomorrow. Goodbye."

Dazed, she hung up the telephone.

"What'd he say? What'd he say?" Jennifer demanded.

"I couldn't hear a thing," Binky complained. "Why was Brock calling you?"

Lexi sat down on the edge of a chair, her arms limp at her sides. "Apparently, his old school is a few weeks behind Cedar River's. He wants to do some extra work so he can catch up and he's asked me to help him."

"You're going to be his tutor?" Peggy gasped.

Jennifer groaned and hit her head with the heel of her hand. "I wish I were smart. If I weren't dyslexic, maybe Brock would have asked *me* to help him with his homework."

"This puts a whole new spin on the idea of studying," Binky said thoughtfully. "Although, I'm not sure how much studying I'd get done with a guy like that sitting across from me."

"Stop it! I'm just helping him as a favor."

"Of all the people in our class that he could have asked to help him with his homework, he picked *you*. That means something, don't you think?"

"It means nothing. The teachers gave him a list of names and he chose mine, that's all."

"That's *enough!* He chose you. He likes you, Lexi. He definitely likes you."

"Does not," Lexi protested.

"It's obvious," Jennifer said. "If he'd wanted just anybody to help him with his homework, he could have picked Tim Anders. Tim's really smart. There are lots of smart people in our class, Lexi. But there's only one of you."

"Quit it, all of you!" Lexi was growing agitated. "You're talking as if he asked me out on a date instead of for help with his homework."

"It sounds like a date to me," Binky said.

"Face it, Lexi, this homework thing is just an excuse. Anyone could see through that in a minute."

"You don't even know him. What if his grades mean a lot to him? Maybe you're misjudging him."

"I've seen the way he's looked at you in school. You're cute, Lexi. He'd be crazy *not* to notice."

Lexi was horrified. Maybe she'd answered Brock too quickly. She should have taken time to think before giving him her decision. She didn't mind helping him and she was willing to be his friend, but suddenly this was beginning to feel like a big mistake.

Agreeing to tutor Brock felt a good deal like betraying Todd.

Chapter Five

There were butterflies the size of birds beating their wings inside Lexi's stomach as she rang the doorbell to Brock's house. She couldn't ever remember being as nervous as she was at this moment. *This is no big deal*, she reminded herself. *No big deal at all.*

She'd almost convinced herself when Brock threw open the door and invited her inside.

He was dressed in blue jeans and a white T-shirt. His dark hair tumbled across one eye and his grin was wide. "Come in. I've been waiting for you."

Curious, Lexi looked around as she stepped inside.

The Taylors' house was an unusual change from the homes to which Lexi was accustomed. The decorating was sleek, stark, and modern. A large futon, two canvas sling chairs, and a large-screen television were the only furniture in the living room. A dramatic modern painting in bright primary colors hung on the wall. The entire house was decorated in minimalist style.

"My mom's a sculptor," Brock said by way of explanation. "She hasn't unpacked any of her work yet. The room won't look so empty when she gets done."

"A sculptor?" Lexi's interest was piqued. "My mother paints."

"We'll have to introduce them. Mom's pleased about our move to Cedar River because this house has room for a studio. She has lots of commissions and wants a place to work without interruption."

"Is she famous?"

"Oh no, she's just my mom." Brock pointed to a magazine laying open on the futon. "There are photos of her work. Take a look if you want."

Lexi was impressed. It appeared that Brock's mother actually *was* a well-known sculptor.

"She'll be up to start dinner soon," Brock said. "Then I'll introduce you. I have my books laid out in the dining room."

Lexi followed him through the house, uncomfortably aware of his broad shoulders and swaggering gait. It felt odd to be noticing this about anyone but Todd.

"I think it's great that you could come this afternoon, Lexi." Brock swung one leg over the top of a dining room chair and dropped into the seat.

"I can only stay until suppertime, but I thought you might want to get started."

"It will give me something to do this evening. My social life has been pretty quiet since we moved."

A little arrow of guilt embedded itself in Lexi's conscience. She hadn't been able to find Todd to tell him her plans for after school. She'd missed their shared classes today because of a dental appointment. Still, it shouldn't matter to Todd that she was tutoring Brock. It wasn't as if they were married or anything. Todd had never demanded to know where Lexi was every moment of the day. Besides, this visit was purely business.

It was not long, however, before Lexi realized that even though *she* considered this visit business, Brock regarded it as something more.

He had soda and snacks set out on a tray on the dining room table and spent time making sure Lexi was comfortable.

"Do you want me to open that drape a little more? Do you need more light? How about a different chair?"

"It's fine, Brock. *Everything* is fine. Let's quit worrying about the drapes and get to work."

"Sorry. It's just that I really appreciate you coming all the way over here tonight. I want to make sure you're comfortable."

"Believe me, I've studied in worse conditions than these," Lexi joked weakly. "Let's get started."

They'd been working over an hour when a slim, youthful woman with long, dark hair drifted into the room. She wore a bodysuit, multicolored skirt, and thick sandals.

"Brock, have you seen my camera? I want to take a picture of the piece I'm working on before I go any further. I looked through three or four boxes and it's nowhere to be found. . . . Oh, hello!"

Lexi found eyes the same amazing turquoise color as Brock's beaming down at her.

"You must be Lexi." The woman thrust out her hand. "I'm Brock's mother."

The woman sat down in a chair across from Lexi and tucked her legs beneath her.

"Brock's told me all about you."

"He has?"

"He says you're very intelligent and that several teachers recommended he ask you to help him catch up at school. He also said that you were attractive." The woman smiled and winked at her son. "I think he's right on both counts."

"Thank you, but . . ."

Mrs. Taylor waved her hand in the air. "Oh, don't be modest. I'm glad you're here to help my son. He wasn't completely delighted about making this move, so it pleases me to know he's finding friends in Cedar River."

"It's hard to make a move while you're in high school," Lexi said sympathetically. "I moved here a year and a half ago. It's difficult to leave your friends behind. Fortunately there are a lot of nice people here in Cedar River. I don't miss Grover's Point much at all anymore."

"See, I told you so," Mrs. Taylor smiled at Brock. "Isn't that good to hear?" Mrs. Taylor perched on the chair like a forest elf who might scamper away at any moment.

"Brock says you're a sculptor," Lexi ventured. "My mother does some painting."

"Does she? How wonderful. I'll have to send my business card home with you. I'd like to meet her."

Mrs. Taylor slipped off the chair and drifted toward the kitchen. "Think I forgot to eat lunch," she said. "So if you two will excuse me, I'm going to start supper. Don't let me interfere with your work."

Brock chuckled as his mom meandered away. "Mom forgets everything when she's working on a project. We're used to reminding her where she's left her shoes and when it's time to sleep. Other than being a little scattered, she's great."

As they worked together, Lexi discovered that it was easy to talk to Brock. He was knowledgeable about a wide range of topics.

"We aren't getting much done."

"That's okay. What we don't get done today, we'll do tomorrow or the next day."

Lexi was a little uncomfortable with the agenda Brock had set for them. This afternoon felt more like a date than a study session. The more quickly she could get Brock up to speed in his classes, the better it would be.

As they closed the textbooks and notebooks that surrounded them, Brock grinned at Lexi. "We work well together, Lexi. A good team."

"It's a start. How does Cedar River compare to your previous school?"

"It's going to take a while to get used to a new place. In my old school, I was captain of the football team, a wrestler, and a debater. It will take time to find places for me at this school. I should be accustomed to moving by now. Both my parents like change. Dad is a military man, so his job has taken him all over the country. I've never really minded until this last move."

"Are you an only child?"

"I have a brother who is two years older than I am. He's in college."

"It must get lonely. . . ."

"Not too bad. Military kids get pretty self-sufficient. Dad taught me to hunt and to play golf so I could do those things with him. He's an astronomy buff too. We've got a big telescope that Dad and I use to study the stars."

"It sounds as though you and your father are close."

"We're cut from the same cloth, according to my mother." Brock grinned. "She usually says that when she's mad at one of us."

"You must like science if you like astronomy."

"I do. And I *don't* like poetry. You'll have to help me a lot with my English assignments."

Lexi enjoyed watching Brock speak. His eyes sparkled when he talked about weight lifting—his favorite hobby—and he grimaced when he talked about leaving his grandparents behind in this last move. Lexi was drawn to the attractive way his forehead wrinkled when he was thinking and the strong cut of his jawline.

"Are you getting bored listening to me talk about myself?" he asked suddenly. "If you are, say so."

"Not at all. I do have a question for you, though, if you don't mind." An idea had occurred to Lexi and she wanted to pursue it further. "Since you like studying the stars—astronomy—do you know anything about astrology?"

"That's weird stuff, isn't it? Planning your life by the stars?"

"Something like that. Some people believe that our destinies are determined by the positions of the stars."

"I'm not big on religion of any kind, but that's too far out to even consider. Why do you ask?" He leaned over to touch Lexi's hand. She felt an unexpected thrill bolt up her arm.

"Oh, never mind." Lexi didn't want to mar the moment with conflict. She would pursue the questions that had arisen later—when Brock's presence wasn't clouding her thinking.

Brock's mother walked into the dining room wiping her hands on a dish towel. "How's the studying progressing?" She put one hand on Brock's shoulder and peered over the top of his head at the books littering the table.

"There's still lots to do, but I'll make it."

"Brock's always been a good student," she assured Lexi. "I can't ever remember having to tell him to study. His brother was a different matter entirely." She shook her head in bewilderment. "How two boys could be so different I'll never know. Brock would study and Brandon would hide assignments under the couch until I vacuumed and discovered them. I was always getting calls from Brandon's teachers telling me that he'd refused to turn in his work or that he was doodling in his books during class time. If I have any gray hairs, Brandon gave them to me."

"But he's in college. He turned out all right," Brock reminded his mother.

Mrs. Taylor's laughter sounded like wind chimes tinkling in the breeze. "Now he's doing what he wants. He's studying art history and taking sketching classes. He's finally able to avoid all those chemistry, physics, and math classes he hated."

"So he's an artist too?" Lexi asked.

"He wants to be. He's a design student right now and he shows great promise. I'm sorry to have to admit it, but all those things that frustrated me about Brandon as a student were the very same things that confounded *my* mother when *I* was a girl. I'm grateful that Brock is more like his father. He doesn't lose track of time when he's trying to sculpt a perfect ear or nose."

There was no doubt in Lexi's mind where Brock had gotten his charm. Though he might not have inherited his mother's artistic tendencies, his personality was much like hers.

"Will you stay for supper, Lexi? We'd love to have you."

Lexi glanced at her watch. "Six-thirty! I didn't realize it was so late." She pushed herself away from the table. "I completely lost track of time."

"Brock has that effect on people," Mrs. Taylor assured Lexi. "And his father has always had that effect on me."

Lexi quickly gathered her books together and shoved them into her backpack. "Thank you for inviting me to stay, but I really do have to go."

"Are you sure?" Brock frowned. "It would be great to have you."

"Maybe another time." For some reason, Lexi did not tell him that she had promised Todd that she would meet him at six. Early in the week they'd made plans for dinner with Todd's brother, Mike. Now she was thirty minutes late!

Lexi was halfway to Mike's garage before she dared to slow down and take a deep breath. What had happened to her? How could she have forgotten her date with Todd? Lexi's stomach churned as she neared the garage.

Would Todd be angry with her? she wondered. Did she dare tell him where she had been?

Chapter Six

Lexi hurried into the garage still clutching her books. Light sifted from beneath the door to Mike's office.

Mike Winston was at his desk bent over a pile of paper work. His dark hair was tousled and he looked tired. The radio droned a country tune in the background.

Todd jumped up from a chair behind the door as she entered. "There you are. I was beginning to worry that we had our signals crossed. I called your house, but no one answered."

"Mom and Dad took Ben to a meeting at the Academy."

"You're usually right on time." Todd's face was furrowed with concern. "We thought something had happened to you."

"I'm sorry. I lost track of time. I'll explain later." Lexi glanced at the clock on the wall. "Mike, do you have a class tonight?"

"I've got a test." He ran his fingers through his already rumpled hair. "Let me give you a piece of advice. Go to college directly from high school. At least you'll be accustomed to taking tests. I've been a wreck studying for this one."

"Are you going to get a degree?" As long as Lexi had known Mike he'd run the garage.

"I think so. I'd like to study business administration or accounting. Dad and I have discussed opening another garage on the other side of Cedar River. When I graduated from high school, I didn't know what I wanted to do with my life, but I loved to work on cars. That's why I went to school to be a mechanic. Now I see that more education would enhance what I like to do . . . if I can pass this test, that is."

Lexi apologized again as they drove to a fast-food restaurant near the garage. "I'm sorry I was so late. Now you'll end up choking down your food and barely make it to class."

"That's okay," Mike said. "It's still nice to have someone to eat dinner with once in a while."

Lexi looked at him sympathetically. "How's it going, Mike? Really, I mean." Mike's fiancee, Nancy, had died of complications from AIDS. Though he never complained, Lexi and Todd both knew there was a dreadful void in Mike's life.

Mike thoughtfully stirred at his drink with his straw. "I think Nancy would like the idea that I'm going back to school. She was big on education. I feel as though I'm doing it for her as well as for myself. Though you couldn't have convinced me of this on the day I graduated from high school, I've discovered that I actually *like* school. I guess I just needed some time to grow up."

"Do you think you'll go full time?"

"Time will tell. Ed prefers that I do the bookwork and I prefer that he work on cars." Mike referred to Ed Bell, his full-time employee.

"Ed's excited about the idea of my going back to school. He says he can envision a whole string of garages in my future. He's been writing jingles for the radio, advertising our business. Who knows? Maybe Ed will go back to school next, to become our public relations man."

It was a terrific thought. When Mike had hired him, Ed couldn't read. Recently, Ed had found a tutor to help him work toward his GED.

"Maybe Ed could go to school *with* you," Todd suggested. "You could help each other study."

"Thanks for the enthusiasm and the encouragement, but don't get too carried away. Pretty soon you'll have us working on our Ph.D.'s in physics."

"And what am I doing talking about physics when I won't even pass the class I'm taking right now if I don't get there for the test? I've got to go. Thanks for the company." Mike crumpled his paper cup and picked up his tray. Todd looked at Lexi and smiled. "Ice cream? *I'm* in no hurry."

"Sure, why not?"

Todd returned with the cones. They were quiet as they ate, neither feeling the need to speak. That was one of the things Lexi liked best about Todd. She could always be herself when she was with him. If she didn't feel like talking, he was comfortable with her silence.

"So, why were you late, Lexi?"

She'd almost forgotten. Even now she couldn't understand why she felt so guilty about it. If Binky and Egg or Peggy had held her up, she'd make no excuses—but because it was Brock she felt as though she'd done something wrong. Even so, there were no lies or secrets between her and Todd. Lexi took a deep breath and plunged into her explanation.

"Brock Taylor wanted me to come to his house and help him with assignments."

Todd arched one eyebrow but said nothing.

"He's behind in his classes because of the move. His teachers recommended that he get help to catch up. Some of them gave him my name. I could hardly say no, could I?" Lexi regretted the defensive tone in her voice.

Todd still said nothing.

"I met his mother. She sculpts. I think my mother would enjoy meeting her." Lexi felt as if she were babbling.

Todd frowned.

"His mother is very young looking—just like a kid herself. Their house is contemporary with hardly a thing in it yet. Brock says his mom has lots of sculptures to put on display."

"That's what you discussed when you were supposed to be studying?" Todd's tone was mild, but there was an odd expression on his face.

"No. It just came up. We covered a lot of subjects. That was one of them."

"Which teachers recommended you?" Todd asked.

"I don't know. Brock didn't say."

"Weren't you curious?"

"Not really. I thought it was flattering." Lexi gave a lopsided grin. "I didn't realize my teachers thought I was such a good student."

"You're always on the honor roll." Todd was behaving very strangely. The expression in his eyes was somber.

"Is something bothering you, Todd?"

"It just seems weird that Brock would ask you to help him and not tell you which teachers recommended it."

"Why?" Lexi felt herself bristling. "Don't you think I'm capable of helping him?"

"That's not what I meant and you know it."

"Then what *did* you mean?"

"Nothing, I guess." Todd pushed at the pile of napkins in front of him. "Forget I said anything at all."

"You don't like the idea of my going to Brock's house, do you?"

Todd dropped his chin toward his chest and refused to look at her.

"That's it, isn't it? You're upset because I went to Brock's."

"It bugs me a little."

"Why? You'd have done the same thing if he'd asked you to help him."

A flush crept up Todd's neck and for the first time Lexi realized just how upset Todd actually was.

"That's different, Lexi."

"What's different?" She suddenly felt defensive and unsure.

"Get real, Lexi. Think about it." Todd spoke sharply. "If you were Brock, who would you rather study with? A great-looking girl or me?"

Lexi was so startled by the statement that she burst out laughing. "Thanks for the compliment, I think. Ease up, Todd! It was no big deal. I only went to his house to help him with some homework. You're acting crazy. . . ." She stared at Todd as a startling notion occurred to her. "You're *jealous*!"

Todd's handsome features flushed. "We just talked about your being my girlfriend, Lexi. How do you think it feels to have that conversation and then, within a matter of days, hear you've gone off to help some new guy in school with his homework? What if he made up that stuff about teachers *recommending* you? Maybe he just picked you out and wanted you to help him. Did you ever think of that?"

This unexpected twist left Lexi speechless. Todd wasn't the jealous type . . . at least he *hadn't* been . . . until now.

"There's nothing for you to be concerned about. Brock and I are friends, that's all."

"Friends already? That happened quickly."

"It's possible," Lexi defended herself. "After all, you and I were friends from the very first time we met. . . ." She knew even as she spoke that she'd chosen the wrong example.

Todd's expression was grim. "That's *exactly* what I meant, Lexi."

"You aren't giving me any credit, Todd Winston!" Lexi felt hurt and angry. "What do you think I am? A big dummy, easily impressed by a guy's attention?"

"Just forget it."

"No, I can't forget it. I've never seen you jealous before."

"Maybe I've never had a reason to *be* jealous before," he retorted.

"You think I'm giving you reason because I agreed to help Brock?" Lexi realized her voice was pitching higher and higher, but she couldn't seem to help it. Two small children in a nearby booth turned to stare at her.

"He's been paying a lot of attention to you. I've watched the way he looks at you in school. Maybe you don't see it, but I do."

"Are you sure you're not imagining these *looks*?"

"Maybe I am, but then Egg's imagining them too. So are Matt and Jerry."

"You've been talking to them about this?" Lexi was furious. "Whatever happened to talking to *me* about things that have to do with me?"

"I'm talking to you right now and it's not working out very well, is it?"

There was truth in Todd's statement, but Lexi felt angry, hurt, and confused. It was as though her temper and her tongue had taken on a will of their own.

"You don't own me, Todd. You never have. I'm not your possession. If I want to help someone with their homework, I will. Anyone I choose. And I'd appreciate it if you wouldn't discuss our problems with your friends before you discuss them with me."

With a vicious thrust, Todd crumpled his cup. Bits of ice splattered onto the tabletop. "Maybe I'd better take you home."

"I think that's a good idea." Lexi walked straight and tall toward the exit, but her legs trembled and tears stung the backs of her eyes.

Always a gentleman, Todd opened the door of his vintage car for her, but his expression was grim. Neither spoke on the short drive to the Leighton house. The atmosphere was thick with tension. Still, Lexi couldn't bring herself to apologize for whatever imagined wrongdoing Todd felt she'd committed. Her pride kept her head high and the words that would have eased the tension locked in her throat.

"Thanks for the ride," she managed when they arrived at her driveway.

"Sure, anytime."

"Guess I better go inside."

"Right."

With all her heart, Lexi wanted to invite Todd into the house to visit Ben and play with Wiggles, but she couldn't manage the words. Pride held her still as she watched Todd drive away.

A verse she'd learned years ago in Sunday school whirled through her brain. *"Pride goes before destruction and haughtiness before a fall."*

Lexi felt dreadful. If being right about something was so desirable, then why did it make her feel so awful? How had their fight happened? It had come out of the blue like a lightning bolt, striking when they'd least expected it. Was it only a few days ago that they were discussing the idea of going steady? Or was that part of the problem?

"Oh, Brock," she murmured, "I wish you'd never come to town."

But as Lexi turned to walk toward her house she knew in her heart that her statement was not true. Brock Taylor was a great guy—handsome, intelligent, funny, easy to be with. Why *shouldn't* he move to town? Why *couldn't* she be friends with both Brock and Todd? She was more confused than she'd been in a long, long time.

"You wanted to see us?" Jennifer, Peggy, Binky,

and Angela stood on the front steps of Lexi's house.

"Come in."

"What's up? You sounded serious when you called." Angela looked concerned. "I made Egg go home after your phone call. I told him you needed me worse than he did."

Angela and Egg had been dating off and on for the past few months. They'd first met while Angela was living at the homeless shelter with her mother. Compassionate Egg had been very sympathetic when he'd discovered that Angela and her mother were temporarily homeless. It was the bond that had drawn the two together.

"What's up?" Jennifer demanded. "You sounded as though you were going to cry on the telephone."

"I need to you to tell me whether or not I'm going crazy."

"That's not likely," Binky snorted. "I live with Egg and *I'm* not going crazy. If it hasn't happened to me, then it certainly won't happen to you."

Lexi smiled weakly. "Egg can drive a person crazy, but so can Brock and Todd."

Peggy's eyebrows lifted so high they nearly disappeared under her auburn hair. "Tell us more. This sounds interesting."

Miserably Lexi blurted out the story of Brock's invitation to study and of Todd's reaction. When she was done, Jennifer whistled.

"Todd—jealous. That doesn't sound like him," Binky blurted.

"Brock brings out the worst in him. Todd thinks he sees something between us that's not there."

"Are you *sure* it's not there?" Angela asked softly. "My mom says that occasionally you meet a person with whom you seem to connect on a different level. You have an easier time understanding each other and an easier time laughing—it's 'chemistry.' "

"I suppose there *is* some of that between Brock and me," Lexi admitted. "He's a neat guy. His mom is an artist just like mine. And he does have great eyes."

"See what I mean?" Angela said. "There *is* a chemistry between the two of you. Frankly, Lexi, even I noticed it. Sometimes in class Brock stares at you like a love-sick puppy. Once I even watched him doodle your name in the back of his notebook."

"Oh, come off it, Angela!"

"It's true—honestly. You may not feel the chemistry as much as he does, but it's definitely there. Todd's no dummy. He'd be blind not to see it."

"What should I *do*?" Lexi wailed. "I'm so confused. The *last* person in the world I want to hurt is Todd. Yet I don't feel he has a right to be angry with me. He doesn't own me. Even if what you say *is* true, I can't help it that Brock stares at me in class. It's not my fault. I haven't done anything wrong."

She looked at Jennifer. "Do *you* think Todd has a right to be angry at me?"

"You *have* dated him for a long time," Jennifer said softly.

"Does that mean that I should tell Brock to find someone else to help him with his schoolwork?"

"Sounds a little bit like wimping out," Binky admitted.

"Then I should continue to help him?"

"I don't know." Binky made a face. "This is too complicated for me."

"Todd doesn't own you," Angela said. "No one can own another person. The only way a relationship works is if people respect and trust each other."

"Don't you think Lexi owes something to Todd?" Peggy mused. "They've been good friends for a long time. Maybe he's hurt because she didn't talk to him first."

"Why does Lexi have to talk to Todd about everything before she does it?" Jennifer wondered aloud. "They aren't married!"

"Should I quit helping Brock or not?" Lexi demanded.

"I don't know." Binky threw her hands in the air. "I'm glad this is your problem and not mine."

Lexi groaned and sank into a chair. "I don't *want* this to be my problem. Todd is the greatest guy in the world. I don't understand why he's making such a big deal of this."

"He's afraid he's going to lose you, Lexi." Angela was blunt.

"Don't do this to me!" Lexi blurted. "I called you here to *help* me figure out what to do. This is just making things worse. Now I feel *really* awful!"

At that moment, Ben and Wiggles burst into the living room.

"Wiggles and I are going for a walk," Ben announced.

"You can't leave the yard with him," Lexi warned. "You know what Mom and Dad said."

"They said 'just the sidewalk in front of our house and the backyard,' " Ben parroted.

"And watch for cars. Hold on to the puppy and don't pull too hard on the leash or you'll choke him."

Ben looked worriedly at Wiggles. The pup had plopped down on the carpet and was chewing on his own hind foot. "I'll take care of him, Lexi. You don't have to worry about *us*." With that confident pronouncement, Ben hauled Wiggles toward the front door.

"I'm glad there's *one* thing I don't have to worry about," Lexi muttered. "Everything else in my life is topsy turvy."

"Sorry we couldn't help," Jennifer said. "I don't know what else to tell you."

"It's so hard!" Lexi moaned. "My parents love Todd. He's like a son to them. Yet, they've never encouraged me to go steady with just one guy. Mom's admitted that Todd is the greatest guy in the world, but that she's disappointed that I've never dated other guys. Now Brock appears . . ."

"I should be so lucky as to have these problems," Binky pointed out.

"Gotta go." Angela looked at her watch. "Mom will be waiting for me."

"Us too." Peggy laid a hand on Lexi's arm. "Sorry we weren't more help. You and Todd are two of my favorite people. I'm sorry you're having problems, but I know you can work them out."

"Thanks for the vote of confidence," Lexi said. "I'm not sure I deserve it."

After the girls left, Lexi sat down on the front step and stared at the darkening sky. "Now what?" she wondered aloud.

Would Lexi—*could she?*—risk losing Todd, the finest guy she had ever known, for someone who was almost a total stranger?

Chapter Seven

Lexi had been attempting to study for over an hour with no success. When the phone rang, she was glad for the diversion.

"Hi, Lexi." The warm male voice that came over the line sent a thrill of excitement through her.

"It's Brock. I've finished with those notes you loaned me. I really appreciate it."

"No problem. I was happy to help."

"I'd like to get together again. I have some more questions for you."

"Maybe . . ." Lexi was reluctant, fearful of what Todd's response might be. Brock did not seem to notice.

"Could we do it this weekend?"

"I don't know. . . ."

"I'd like to take you out to thank you for all you've done for me. A movie maybe? Or dinner? Whatever you want."

"That's not necessary. I was happy to, really. You don't need to do anything for me."

"Then I'd like to do it for me. I enjoy your company, Lexi. I'd like to take you out."

This was happening too quickly. Lexi hadn't sorted out her thoughts about her argument with

Todd. Brock's invitation only complicated matters further.

"What do you say, Lexi? This weekend? Are we on?"

"I'm sorry, Brock, I really can't. Not this weekend." Lexi was relieved that she could say no with such honesty. "My parents are going to a veterinarian's conference out of town and I'm staying home with my little brother. He's got a new puppy. Between the two of them, they're going to need a lot of watching."

"Another time, then?"

"We'll see," she said noncommittally.

"Great." It was as though he hadn't noticed the hesitation in her voice at all.

Lexi heard the doorbell ringing in the background at Brock's house.

"Somebody's at the door. Talk to you later."

As she hung up the phone, Lexi groaned. Todd hadn't liked the idea of Lexi helping Brock study. He *certainly* wasn't going to approve of Brock's invitation.

"Are you talking to yourself in here?" Lexi's mother walked into the room wearing jeans, moccasins, and an old shirt of Mr. Leighton's, one that she used for housecleaning and painting.

Mrs. Leighton sat down on the couch and patted the cushion next to her. "Sit down, Lexi. Tell me what's on your mind. You've been walking around the house like a little gray storm cloud. Tell me what's happened to make you look so miserable."

"Has it been that obvious?"

"I'm your mother. I'm accustomed to watching your every mood."

"It's been a lousy week." Lexi flung herself down next to her mother.

Mrs. Leighton curled her legs beneath her and waited for Lexi to continue.

"I'm having boy trouble."

"Most girls do at one time or another."

"Usually a girl's problem is that she doesn't have a boy in her life. I suddenly have too many."

"That's a pleasant switch. Tell me more."

"Things have been just awful between Todd and me lately, Mom. I feel as though I'm losing my best friend. Todd asked me if I wanted to go steady."

"And what did you tell him?" Mrs. Leighton's face was carefully blank.

"I didn't tell him anything. I know you and Dad don't want me to get tied down to one guy, but Todd really is special to me. Before I could give him an answer, something else happened." Lexi told her mother about the arrival of Brock and Todd's response to him.

"We argued about Brock. Now I feel Todd pulling away. He's avoiding me and I don't know what to do about it." Lexi continued. "I don't even know what to say to him anymore! It's so awkward."

"I'm sure it is," Mrs. Leighton said sympathetically. "But you have to understand Todd's side of the situation too."

"*His* side?"

"He's been your friend for a long time. Just after he decided to make a more serious commitment to you, a new boy comes along who's handsome, charming, witty and, from what you've told me, a threat to all the boys in school. No wonder Todd's pulled back! He doesn't want to be hurt. No one does."

"What should I do?"

"I'm not crazy about you having a steady boyfriend, Lexi, but I do believe it's important to be loyal to your friends. It would be a shame if your friendship with Todd were destroyed in this misunderstanding."

"That's what bothers me most of all. Brock's nice and he *is* handsome . . . but there's something very special about my feelings for Todd."

"Perhaps the two of you should talk honestly about what's going on."

"It would be a relief," Lexi admitted. "All I've thought about lately is Todd and Brock. I have questions but no answers."

"I have a suggestion for you," Mrs. Leighton said. "There's a little carnival at the Academy this evening. Ben would love to go. Why don't you ask Todd if he'd like to join you and Ben?"

"That's a great idea! Besides, Ben and I haven't done anything together for a long time."

Lexi gave her mom a hug. "Thanks for listening and not trying to make my decisions for me."

Mrs. Leighton stroked away a strand of hair that had fallen into Lexi's eyes. "That's the hardest thing about being a mother. But I know you'll never learn unless you make decisions for yourself. You're a smart girl, Lexi. You'll work this out."

"I'm going to call Todd right now and ask him if he wants to go to the carnival with us." She grabbed the phone and dialed his number.

"Lexi?" It was obvious Todd had not expected her to call.

"Are you working for Mike tonight?"

"No. He has an appointment with his college counselor to discuss classes."

"He's going through with it then? He's going to keep going to school?"

"Sounds that way. What are *you* up to tonight?"

"Benjamin and I were wondering if you'd like to come with us to the carnival at the Academy tonight?"

"Sure! I mean . . . why not?" Though Todd tried to temper his initial enthusiasm, Lexi could hear the pleasure and excitement in his voice.

"Ben is just about jumping out of his shoes because he is so excited," Lexi admitted. "His face looks like a boiled tomato because he scrubbed it so hard when he was getting ready."

"Give me ten minutes to change clothes and I'll be over," Todd said. "Tell him not to wash his face again until I get there."

Todd was as good as his word. He pulled up in front of Lexi's house just as she and Ben walked out the front door with their mother.

"Hi, big fellow," Ben greeted Todd cheerfully. "Are you taking us to the carnival?"

"Sounds that way."

"Can we take Wiggles with us?"

"Don't answer that, Todd," Mrs. Leighton said with a chuckle. "Ben already knows the answer is no."

"I don't think your dog would like the carnival very well, Ben. He might get stepped on."

"He'll be lonesome without me," Ben worried. "He'll cry if I'm not here."

Mrs. Leighton scratched behind the ear of the

squirming puppy she held under her arm. "Don't worry, Ben. I can handle this dog for a couple hours while you're at the carnival. Don't you think I'm a good mother?"

"But you've never been a *puppy's* mother before," Ben answered cautiously.

"It sure can't be more difficult than taking care of you and Lexi. I raised two children, Ben. This puppy should be no problem."

"Will you call Daddy if you have trouble?" Ben glanced warily at his mother, not convinced she could manage the enormous task before her.

"Promise." Mrs. Leighton ruffled Ben's silky hair. "Wiggles is very fortunate to have such a good master."

"Maybe he could stay in the car."

"No, Ben. You go with Todd and Lexi. Wiggles will be fine. He'll be waiting for you when you get back."

Ben dragged his feet all the way down the sidewalk, but by the time he reached the car, he began chatting animatedly about what he was going to do at the carnival.

The Academy for the Handicapped was a private school for students like Ben. Many of his friends there also had Down's syndrome.

The front gates of the Academy were strung with brightly twinkling lights and the gymnasium was an explosion of color. While Lexi and Todd purchased tickets, Ben raced ahead to the ring toss. He'd already won a balloon and a brightly colored hat with a feather by the time Lexi and Todd reached him.

"You're not supposed to play the games without these tickets, Ben."

"I know, but I told them you were coming and you'd pay for me. See what I won, Lexi? Let's go pick ducks." And Ben was off again.

By the time Lexi and Todd reached the large pool, Ben was busy plucking little yellow plastic ducks out of the water.

They spent the evening drifting from one activity to another—the duck pond, the magician, the nickel toss, the cake walk. More than once Lexi was glad for Ben's laughter and chatter. It helped to dispel the tension that hung between her and Todd like an invisible curtain.

While Lexi stood in line to purchase more tickets, she watched Ben and Todd throw small rubber rings at the necks of soda pop bottles laid in a pattern. She sighed wistfully. Something had changed.

The comfortable comradery she and Todd had always shared was gone. Some intangible barrier had developed between them. Lexi hated the change but knew no way to make it right.

"Good-night, Todd. Thanks for taking me to the carnival."

Ben was droopy-eyed but smiling, his face a sticky mask of cotton candy and chocolate ice cream. He rubbed his hands on the front of his shirt and yawned. "I wish we could go to a carnival every night."

"I'm glad we can't, little fellow," Todd said. "Then it wouldn't be special anymore."

"I suppose," Ben yawned again. "Good-night,

Todd. Good-night, Lexi." Ben disappeared into the house, leaving Lexi and Todd alone on the porch.

"I'm glad you called," Todd said slowly. "That was fun. Ben's a good kid."

"He is, isn't he? You'll have to come over again and see him playing with Wiggles. They're quite a pair."

"I'd like that," Todd said softly.

It was then that Lexi realized just how much things had changed between them. Three weeks ago Todd would not have waited for an invitation to visit Ben and the puppy. Now he was holding back, waiting for an invitation to a place he should have felt welcome.

"Call again, Lexi. Anytime." Todd leaned over and lightly kissed Lexi on the cheek. Before she could move or respond, he turned away and walked down the steps toward his car.

Lexi watched him leave. Her throat ached at the sight of his familiar, athletic walk, his shoulders rolling beneath the cloth of his shirt. She touched her cheek where his lips had been. There was something very sad and final about that kiss.

She leaned her forehead against the coolness of the front door and closed her eyes. The excitement and bright lights of the carnival had not been able to banish the tension between her and Todd. What was going wrong? Was there any way to stop it? Feeling miserable and confused, Lexi went to her room and cried herself to sleep.

Chapter Eight

"Hey, Lexi, wait up." Egg McNaughton was waiting for her at the school entrance.

"Good morning, Egg."

"I want to talk to you. Do you have a minute?"

"Sure." Lexi smiled at her gawky friend. Egg was tall and thin with an Adam's apple that bobbed when he spoke. He was also gangly and slightly goofy looking and one of her dearest friends. "I have to drop a book off at the library. We could talk in there before school."

"Fine. Let's go." Egg picked up his backpack and led the way.

Lexi was startled by his businesslike march toward the library. He usually ambled loose-jointed, like the scarecrow in the *Wizard of Oz*. Today he walked as though he was a man with a mission, with something on his mind.

Lexi set her book on the librarian's desk and then followed Egg to the far corner of the library.

"What's on your mind, Egg?"

"I need to talk to you, Lexi."

"Talk away."

"I don't want you to be mad at me."

"What could you do to make me mad at you?"

"I could butt into your business," Egg said. "But I feel I need to do this to help my friend."

"You'd better explain yourself." Lexi didn't like the sound of this.

"I know that you and Todd have been having troubles."

Lexi's stomach gave a little flip-flop.

"I also know that Todd is really hurt by your friendship with Brock."

"That's none of his business. . . ."

Egg would not be stopped. "Todd feels pushed out. He thinks he's been replaced."

"That's not *true*, Egg! I'm just helping Brock with his homework—nothing else."

"Nothing? Are you sure? You mean he hasn't asked you out?"

"No!" Lexi paused. "At least not exactly . . . maybe sort of."

"Sort of? Brock *sort of* asked you out?"

"He's new, Egg, that's all. It's no big deal. What's going on with everyone?" Lexi felt hurt, frustrated, and a little afraid.

"I'm wondering how you'd feel if the shoe were on the other foot, that's all. What if a cute little brunette with big blue eyes moved to Cedar River and decided that Todd was the only guy in school who could help her with her homework? Wouldn't it bother you?"

Lexi paused to imagine it. "Yes, I suppose it would, but I'd know that it was silly to worry. I'd know that Todd cared for me."

"That would be your *head* thinking, Lexi. How about your *heart*?"

There was no way Lexi could argue. Her head

and her heart hadn't been agreeing on a lot of things lately.

"I want to be friends with *both* Todd and Brock. I don't want to change anything I have with Todd, but I don't think I should have to refuse Brock's friendship either. Friends shouldn't be an 'either or' proposition, should they?"

"Not always, but sometimes," Egg said bluntly. "I think you're being unrealistic. It's obvious to everyone except you that Brock wants you as *more* than just a friend. He wants you as a girlfriend, Lexi. He said as much to Tim before he realized Tim was a good friend of Todd's."

"He said that?"

"He told Tim that he thought Lexi Leighton was really 'hot' and that he'd like to go out with her. That's more than helping with homework, if you ask me."

"That's not my fault, Egg. I can't help what he says to other people."

"True, but you can't stand on the fence forever either. Three's a crowd, Lexi, and sooner or later you're going to have to decide between Todd and Brock."

"Why is it that everyone thinks we have to pair up as if we're heading onto Noah's ark? Can't anyone act like an adult around this school? There's no reason that my friendship with Brock should hurt my relationship with Todd."

"Good luck, Lexi. That's a great idea, but I don't think you can do it. Someday it's going to boil down to this: you'll have to choose between Todd and Brock. It's coming whether you want to admit it or not."

"Did Todd tell you this?"

"Todd hasn't said anything. But I can tell he is afraid—afraid of losing you."

"Why does friendship have to be so complicated?"

"I don't know. It just is, I guess. I'm sorry if you consider this butting in, Lexi, but I really wanted to talk to you."

"Thanks for caring. I don't agree with you, but I do appreciate what you're trying to do. Todd and I are lucky to have a friend like you."

Egg grabbed Lexi's hand and held it tight. "I'm selfish too. I don't want my life to change. We've had a lot of fun times together, Lexi. Haven't we?"

"Don't talk like our good times are in the past, Egg," Lexi pleaded. "We're going to have a lot more."

"Not if Brock has anything to say about it."

"We'll work it out, Egg. It will be okay. I promise."

Egg looked sad. "Don't make promises you can't keep."

"You don't have much faith in me, do you?"

"It's not that," Egg admitted. "But I know my friend. Todd's hurt. He feels pushed out. Brock's intentionally doing it whether you realize it or not. Frankly, if this goes on much longer, I don't know what Todd's going to do."

"Todd and I took Ben to the carnival at the Academy last night. We talked. Everything's going to be fine." Even as Lexi said the words, she wasn't sure she believed them.

"We'll work it out," she rushed on. "All Todd and I need to do is communicate a little better. We haven't been very good at that lately. That's my fault. Sometimes when I'm not sure what to say, I don't say anything. Maybe Todd's been getting the wrong messages about me and Brock because I've been so quiet."

Egg looked a little more hopeful. "You'll talk to him and get this straightened out?"

"I promise. It's the first thing on my agenda for after school tonight, all right?"

"Thanks, Lexi. I don't want anything to ever break up our gang."

All day Lexi thought about Egg's concerns. Maybe he was right. She and Todd had to deal with this thing straight on and talk it out. Perhaps Brock *was* getting in the way of their friendship and Todd was more hurt than she'd realized.

She was eager to find Todd after school but by the time she arrived at her locker, he was nowhere in sight.

"Have you seen Todd?"

Tressa and Gina Williams shared an odd look. "He left right after school. He was on his way to the Hamburger Shack."

"Great, I'll find him there. Thanks." Lexi took no notice of the smirk on Tressa's face or the warning glare Tressa gave her sister when Gina started to speak.

All Lexi could think about on the way to the Hamburger Shack was Todd. They would straighten things out once and for all. If that meant never seeing Brock again, then that's the way it would be. She refused to lose her best friend over a boy she barely knew.

Her decision made, and feeling better than she

had in days, Lexi hurried into the Hamburger Shack. Todd was sitting at the corner table, the one he usually shared with Lexi and their friends.

She'd almost reached them when Lexi realized that Todd was not alone. Todd's attention was focused on the girl across from him.

Chapter Nine

Todd was laughing. His blue eyes lit with warmth and affection, expressions Lexi had believed he'd reserved only for her. Lexi thought she'd seen the attractive blonde with some of the sophomores, but she wasn't sure. The girl was obviously enchanted by his attention. Her hand fluttered out to touch Todd's arm as it rested on the table. The remains of a shared banana split were on the table between them.

Lexi stopped as short as if she'd run full force into a glass wall; an unseen fist of emotion punched through her stomach. Seeing him and the girl in "their" booth, sharing a banana split as she and Todd so often had, caused tears of betrayal to flood her eyes.

Along with betrayal came another emotion, one equally uncomfortable and disturbing—guilt.

She stepped behind a divider that separated the entrance from the main serving room and stared at them, looking—really looking—at Todd for the first time in several weeks. Maybe she'd begun to take him for granted lately—his charm, his handsome good looks, his ever-ready smile. Now, seeing Todd through the eyes of the girl across from him, Lexi realized she'd made a terrible mistake.

Slow down, Leighton. She steadied herself on a nearby stool. *You don't even know why they're together. A class project maybe or . . .* "Who are you fooling?" she wondered aloud.

The pretty blonde was blatantly flirting with Todd and he was enjoying it.

Lexi wanted desperately to walk to the table and calmly inquire what they were doing, but it was impossible. Her emotions had gone ballistic. Tears threatened and her throat constricted. Her stomach was taking a roller-coaster ride and her legs and arms were trembling. Betrayed by her own emotions and by Todd, she turned and ran.

Not far from her house, Lexi stumbled on a broken spot in the pavement. She would have fallen if she had not sprawled directly into Egg McNaughton's arms.

Egg looked as startled as she. "Whoa! Going out for the Olympics? You'd better be careful. You'd have broken something if I hadn't been here to catch you."

Egg had a firm grip on Lexi's upper arms as he set her upright, then frowned into her face. "Lexi, are you crying?"

"Thanks for catching me. Now go away."

Egg's comical face twisted into a mask of mock outrage. "If that's the kind of hero's thanks I get, I'm going to give up being a knight in shining armor entirely."

"I'm sorry, Egg. I didn't mean it the way it sounded. I just don't want to talk right now."

"Obviously." He propped his fists on his skinny hips. "As my sister often tells you, I don't take directions very well. I'm not leaving until you tell me what's wrong."

"Not now, Egg . . . please."

"I think *now* is just fine." Egg grabbed Lexi by the arm and pulled her toward a bus bench. "Sit down and tell Uncle Egg what's the matter."

"I don't want to talk about it. It's nothing."

"Right. *Nothing* makes Lexi Leighton cry. Something has happened and I want to know what it is."

"It's none of . . ."

"I know, I know . . . none of my business," Egg finished for her. "Well, I'm making it my business. You're one of my best friends, Lexi. I'm not going to give up. You might as well spill the beans."

"It's Todd," Lexi blurted, unable to contain herself.

"What about him? Is he hurt? Sick? Moving out of the country?"

"I was just at the Hamburger Shack and I saw him with another girl."

"Really?" Egg looked interested, but not surprised.

"How could he *do* that to me, Egg? They were sitting at *our* booth sharing a banana split. That's what *we* always did. I feel like I caught him cheating on me!"

Egg made some sympathetic clucking noises, but otherwise did not seem terribly shocked or sympathetic. "Are you and Todd going steady?" he inquired mildly, although he knew the answer perfectly well already.

"No, but . . ."

"Then he has every right to be in the Hamburger Shack with whomever he wants, right?"

"I suppose, but . . ."

"You and Todd never agreed to save that booth or banana splits just for the two of you, did you?"

"Of course not!" Lexi had expected Egg to be sympathetic to her plight. Instead, Egg was making her feel even worse.

"After all," he continued, "you've only gotten what you asked for."

"What?" Lexi stared at Egg, dumbfounded.

"Now you know how *Todd* feels when he sees you with Brock," Egg said bluntly. "Seems to me that you don't have a right to complain about Todd when he's with another girl, if he doesn't have the right to be annoyed at you for spending time with Brock. If Todd can't depend on you to be around, maybe it's a good idea for him to make some new friends."

Lexi sagged limply against the bench, stunned by Egg's bluntness. Humiliation, anger, and confusion raced through her. "I thought you were my friend, Egg!"

"I *am* your friend. That's why I'm being honest. You've hurt Todd and don't even realize it."

"I'm not hurting him. He's hurt *me*."

"It works both ways, Lexi." Egg didn't waver from his opinion. "Think about it."

"I don't have to think about it. I already know what I think." She stood up and dusted off her jeans. "Thanks for nothing, Egg."

"Lexi, I . . ." Egg began, but Lexi walked away, her head held high, tears streaming down her cheeks.

It took some effort, but Lexi managed to avoid her friends for the rest of the week.

It was Ben who first complained about the change in his sister.

"Want to play with Wiggles and me?" He held a soggy green tennis ball in his hand. "Wiggles plays fetch really good, Lexi. It'll be fun."

"No thanks, Ben, not now."

"When then?"

"I don't know. Later."

"How much later?"

"Benjamin, I said *not now*."

"But that's what you always say!" Ben stormed, his round face pouty. "You *never* want to play with Wiggles and me."

"I do so. I just haven't lately."

"Lately is forever." Then good-hearted Ben, too sweet to carry a grudge, smiled. "Wanna watch television with us instead?"

Lexi was reprieved by her mother's call to supper.

After grace was said, no one spoke. The table was shrouded in uncomfortable silence. "Lexi, is something wrong?" Dr. Leighton ventured.

"No. Why?"

"You seem listless and depressed lately."

"Your dad and I are worried about you." As Mrs. Leighton passed the mashed potatoes, Lexi noticed that her mother's hands were stained with paint.

"Have you been doing a lot of painting lately?" Lexi attempted to divert the interest away from herself.

"You mean you haven't noticed? I've been in my studio every day."

"Oh."

"That's *exactly* what I'm talking about, young lady. You haven't looked to the right or the left or spoken to anyone unless spoken to all week. It's time to discuss what's wrong."

Lexi shook her head stubbornly. It was too painful and confusing. "I can't."

"Lexi, there are some very important things that you need to remember about your family. First, we're always here for you, no matter what. Second, we'll always listen to what you have to say. We care, Lexi. Give us a chance to prove it."

The compassionate tone of her mother's voice broke the barrier that Lexi had erected.

"My life is falling apart," Lexi announced dramatically.

"Maybe talking about it will help you to put it all into perspective," her mother said, her voice neutral.

"I'm not sure I *want* it in perspective," Lexi admitted. "I might not like what I see."

"Does this have anything to do with the fact that we haven't seen Todd around here all week?" Dr. Leighton asked mildly.

Ben, sensing that this was an adult conversation, carried his plate to the kitchen and disappeared into the backyard.

When Lexi had told her parents everything she stared at her hands as they lay folded in her lap. Finally she looked up. "Aren't you going to lecture me too? You're the ones that told me not to get serious. Aren't you going to say that I've caused my own mess?"

"Lexi, you know what your dad and I think

about tying yourself down too early in life. But I also raised you to think for yourself. I'm very confident of your abilities. So no lectures."

"No advice?"

"Just an expression of confidence, Lexi. Confidence that you will treat both Brock and Todd fairly. Confidence that you will come away from this experience wiser than before."

Lexi groaned and held her head in her hands. "Why is it that when I get what I think I want—like the freedom to make my own decisions—I realize freedom isn't as terrific and wonderful as I thought."

"Do you want us to tell you what to do about this, Lexi? We can, you know. I've got lots of opinions." Her dad was only half joking.

Lexi shook her head. "No, but thanks for listening. I guess that's what I really needed right now. Egg was right. I did treat Todd shabbily. I expected more of him than I was willing to give of myself."

She looked at her parents ruefully. "This is what being an adult is all about, isn't it?"

Lexi's father and mother both nodded, small smiles on their faces.

"Then maybe I don't want to grow up after all."

Being treated as an adult wasn't half the fun she'd expected it to be.

"Good morning." Todd met Lexi at her locker as she retrieved books for her first class. One thing that had come of her conversation with her parents was a decision not to avoid her friends anymore. It wasn't solving anything or making her feel any happier.

As they walked down the hall together, Lexi could almost pretend that the past couple weeks had never happened—until the blonde she'd seen in the Hamburger Shack came waltzing down the hall in the opposite direction.

"Good morning, Todd!"

Lexi winced at the girl's enthusiastic greeting. She looked as though she were about to explode into a series of cartwheels.

"Hi, Molly. How's it going today?"

"Great. Will I see you later?"

Much to Lexi's dismay, Todd nodded.

"Who's that?" Lexi asked after the girl had left. She hoped her voice was neutral.

"I should have introduced you. Her name is Molly Kemp. She moved here last summer. She lives with her grandparents, down the block from us."

Lexi felt a desperate sinking sensation in the pit of her stomach. She remembered all too well what it was like to be the new girl in town. She remembered, too, how Minda had liked Todd and how, when Lexi had moved to town, he had become interested in her. For the first time Lexi fully realized how Minda must have felt.

"What are you thinking about?"

"Minda."

"So early in the morning?" Todd looked amused. "Is she giving you a hard time already today?"

"Not at all. I was thinking that perhaps I've misjudged her."

Todd stared at Lexi strangely. He might have

spoken but at that moment Molly, who had turned and followed them down the hall, touched his arm.

"Todd, could you give me a ride home tonight? My grandmother can't pick me up after school. I was just wondering . . ." Molly's voice trailed away in a breathy whisper.

"Sure, no problem."

Molly gave him a bright smile and turned away.

Lexi supposed a request for a ride home was innocent enough. Still, Todd seemed unduly pleased to be asked. Exactly how much was there to this relationship between him and the new girl on his street?

"Thanks for staying after school to help me straighten out these music cabinets," Mrs. Waverly said. "You've made a tiresome job into a pleasant one, Lexi."

"Sure, anytime." Lexi's mind was not on the music she was filing. She'd seen Todd and Molly leave right after school.

Molly was what Jennifer called a "touchy-feely" kind of girl. When she talked she put her hand on Todd's arm. It seemed natural and unforced, but Lexi had a hunch that Molly was a little more "touchy-feely" with Todd than she would have been with Egg or another boy.

Lexi didn't even look up as someone entered the music room.

"There you are!" Lexi lifted her head at the sound of Brock's voice. "I've been looking for you. Hi, Mrs. Waverly."

Mrs. Waverly smiled at Brock. Teachers liked

him. He made a real effort to be friendly with adults around the school.

"I've got enough homework to choke a horse," he announced. "How about you?"

Lexi glanced at her book bag. "Some."

"Do you want to study together? I'll bribe you with pizza if I have to. Half pepperoni, half Canadian bacon and pineapple, all with extra cheese. What do you say?"

Lexi was about to refuse when the memory of Todd and Molly shimmered into her brain. Molly was going to ask Todd to study with her, Lexi felt certain. What's more, she doubted that Todd would refuse.

"Sure, why not?" The barrier building between her and Todd was growing larger and larger.

It was odd to be spending the evening at Brock's house instead of Todd's. Brock's mother drifted through the dining room occasionally, a vacant expression on her face. She was so different from brisk-but-caring Mrs. Winston.

The Taylor house even felt different. Sleek and contemporary, it was very unlike the cozy warmth of the Winstons' home. Lexi could find no argument with Brock, however. He was funny, witty, and charming.

"Are you getting sick of this?" he inquired after an hour or two, nodding toward the school books stacked on the table.

Lexi looked at her wristwatch. "I'd better go. I didn't realize how late it was."

As she reached to gather her books, Brock

grasped her wrist. "I can't let you get away this easily. How about tomorrow night? Don't you think we deserve a reward for all the work we've accomplished?"

"A reward?"

"How about skating?"

"I don't have any skates."

"You can wear my mom's."

"Your mom has in-line skates?"

"As you may have guessed by now, there's not much that's predictable about my mother." His eyes crinkled up at the corners. "Or me either, for that matter. The only thing I can predict about myself right now is that I want to spend more time with you. How about it? Skating at seven?"

Reluctantly Lexi nodded. Maybe it wasn't wise, but it felt good to have someone so interested in her—especially now that Todd was drifting away.

Chapter Ten

"You're going out again tonight?" Ben stood in the doorway of Lexi's bedroom with Wiggles under one arm. "Last night you went in-line skating. Wiggles and I wanted to wait up for you, but Mom made us go to bed."

"I'll play with you and Wiggles soon."

"We miss you, Lexi." Ben's lower lip trembled.

"You can't miss me when I'm not going anywhere."

"You're going somewhere right now," Ben pointed out with flawless logic.

"Don't do this to me, Ben, not now. Brock will be here any second."

At that moment Lexi heard a horn honk outside. Her mother stood at the front door, one eyebrow raised skeptically.

"Why are you looking like that, Mom?"

"Doesn't this young man know how to walk up the steps and ring the doorbell?"

Lexi had been thinking the same thing, but now that her mother had gently criticized Brock, she felt obliged to defend him.

"Just because he didn't come to the door doesn't mean he isn't nice, Mom."

"I didn't say that, Lexi. But you do know my opinion about manners."

"I know, I know. You don't approve of honking as an alternative for ringing the doorbell and coming inside to say hello."

Mrs. Leighton's grin turned impish. "Do you want me to go outside and give him a motherly lecture?"

"Thanks, but no thanks." Lexi smiled as she leaned to give her mother a kiss on the cheek. "I won't be late. Good-night."

As she walked down the sidewalk toward the car, Lexi attempted to devise a way to tell Brock the honk-and-wait method of picking her up was not well received at her house. She forgot about it, however, the moment she slipped into Brock's car and was handed a single yellow rose.

"Brock, how beautiful! What's this for?"

"A perfect rose for a perfect girl, that's all."

Lexi buried her nose in the petals and inhaled deeply.

She would quit comparing Brock to Todd, she vowed. Brock's manners might be different than Todd's, but he was still a gentleman. Wasn't the rose proof of that?

They headed toward the fairgrounds outside of town. Soon Lexi could smell peanuts roasting and see a cotton-candy booth. The woman inside the cotton-candy booth was spinning huge pink wads of sugar into a cottony mass.

They walked down the midway, stopping often so Brock could try the games of chance. Barkers yelled at them as they passed.

"Hey, mister, bring your girlfriend over here. Win her a teddy bear."

"Do you want one?" Brock turned to Lexi.

"That's not necessary. You can't win anyway. My dad says it's cheaper to buy a stuffed animal than it is to attempt to win one at a carnival."

"This is more fun. Come on." Brock drew Lexi closer to the booth where the man who'd called out to them stood.

The carnival barker was deftly juggling balls in the air. "Knock over three bottles and you can have this teddy bear." He pointed a filthy fingernail toward a ratty-looking teddy bear with a purple bow around its neck.

"Brock, I don't think you should . . ."

"Shh, Lexi, let me try."

Fifteen minutes later Brock's expression had gone from pleasant to determined and Lexi was getting nervous. She'd lost track of how many times he'd put money down on the counter to buy more balls. The game had become a thing of principle with him. He *wanted* that teddy bear and appeared willing to spend whatever it cost to get it.

"Brock, don't. . . ."

"Quiet, Lexi." He shrugged. "This is going to be it."

Lexi was surprised and hurt.

Who's he trying to win this teddy bear for anyway?

A whoop of triumph broke into her thoughts as an elusive bottle tumbled over.

"You won your lady a teddy bear, mister. Good job." The man pulled the ratty teddy bear off the wall and handed it to Brock.

Brock shook his head. "I want the big one."

"Gotta knock over more bottles to get that one, mister."

"Fine. I want the big one."

"Brock, don't."

"Hey, Lexi. I want this for you."

It took several more tries and many more dollars before Brock finally walked away from the booth with a gigantic black and white Panda with a bright red bow.

Lexi wanted to be pleased and excited, but she wasn't. The panda was not worth the embarrassing scene at the booth.

"For you," Brock presented Lexi with the bear.

"Brock, it's not necessary . . ."

"Don't be silly."

"How are we going to get it home?"

"In the backseat of the car. Have you got a place in your room for it?"

"I guess I can make one." Lexi was a little bewildered by his attitude.

Brock was being genuinely kind now, a complete turnaround from his abrupt short-tempered behavior earlier.

Maybe she was overly sensitive. Perhaps his personality just took some getting used to. He had a tendency to push his way to the heads of lines and to be very single-minded about what *he* wanted. More than once she'd caught others glaring at him as he edged and shoved his way to where he wanted to be.

Lexi was almost relieved when Brock suggested that they leave the carnival and find somewhere to eat. Lexi had the beginnings of a headache.

The restaurant they found was quiet and dark. As Brock ordered, she tipped her head forward and massaged the back of her neck with her fingertips.

"Something wrong?"

"Just a headache. It must have been all that excitement winning the teddy bear," Lexi joked weakly.

"My mom says that headaches are *all in your head.* Get it?" Brock appeared to think that his statement was funny. "Actually, she means that headaches come from stress and tension and that you can choose to have headaches or not to have them."

"Something to eat might help," Lexi ventured as the waitress neared.

As their food was placed before them on the table, Brock reached out to grab a fistful of french fries. He was already eating before the last plate was placed on the table.

Lexi hesitated. She was accustomed to prayer before she ate, giving thanks for the gifts she'd been given. It was second nature to her and to her family, and it seemed odd and discordant to be eating with someone who was not accustomed to saying grace before meals. Todd always did. . . .

She bent her head and closed her eyes and said a private grace. When she was done, she sat quietly. She needed to think.

Tonight had been a night of revelation. It was as though she'd seen Brock for the first time. It was so difficult not to compare Brock to Todd.

That was unfair, Lexi reminded herself. Though Todd had good manners and Christian beliefs and attitudes similar to hers, that didn't make him perfect—and everyone else wrong. Maybe this headache was just getting to her. Maybe if she had something to eat. . . .

Lexi was about to reach for a french fry when Brock touched the plate. "If you don't want these, I'll take some."

She pushed the plate toward him. "Go ahead, have them all." She might need to eat but she didn't feel very hungry.

"How's your little brother doing with that puppy?" Brock asked.

"Benjamin adores Wiggles and vice versa. We should have gotten a puppy years ago. I've never seen Ben so happy. Ben's already taught Wiggles to sit. He hasn't had much success with lie down yet, however. That puppy is going to be so spoiled. . . ."

"Is everything all right here?" the waitress asked pleasantly as she passed the table.

Lexi nodded but Brock frowned. "The orders of fries are pretty small, aren't they?"

The waitress looked surprised. "I'm sorry. If you'd wanted more, we also offer a large-sized serving."

"You could have told us in advance," Brock stated grimly.

Lexi felt herself starting to blush.

"Would you like me to bring you another order?"

"It's too late now. We're almost done."

The young waitress looked flustered. "I'm sorry that you were unhappy with the fries. I'll take them off your bill."

"That would be a good idea."

Lexi stared at Brock after the woman had left the table.

"You can't let these people get by with things, you know," he said matter-of-factly. "You'll get stepped all over if you do."

"There were plenty of french fries," Lexi said.

"For you maybe. Not for me." He grinned and the harshness disappeared from his features.

"Look at these, Lexi." He flexed his biceps. "It takes a lot of fuel to keep me going. Don't look so worried. That's what waitresses get paid to do, take orders. It's no skin off her nose if she has to change the bill."

"Sometimes waitresses have to make up for mistakes out of their own paychecks," Lexi pointed out.

"Then she'll tell people about the size of the orders from now on, won't she?" Brock shrugged off the incident as though it were an old shirt. "What do want to do next? Bowling? A walk in the park? You name it. Your wish is my command."

Lexi's head was swimming by the time they left the restaurant with Brock's hand tucked protectively in the small of her back.

In many ways she couldn't have asked for a nicer or sweeter escort. Unfortunately that picture was marred by the flashes of Brock's bruskness and impatience. Todd might have complained to the waitress, but never in that way. . . .

There I go again, comparing Brock and Todd.

It wasn't smart *or* fair to do that. Besides, Brock was here and Todd was somewhere else, probably with another girl.

"Mom asked if you could stop by the house and see what she's working on," Brock said at the end of the evening. "She's doing a series of sculptures about a mother and child."

"I'd like to look at them." Lexi was pleased by the invitation.

All the lights were on at Brock's home as they pulled into the driveway. They could see his father in the living room reading the newspaper and his mother working at the dining room table.

"What are you doing, Mom?" Brock asked as he and Lexi entered.

"Some crystal beads broke off this light fixture in the move. I'm trying to restring them." Mrs. Taylor was working with needle-nosed pliers and fine wire.

"That looks hard," Lexi commented.

"It is and I'm not doing a very good job."

"Maybe Dad could help you . . ." Brock began.

He was cut off by a snorting sound from the living room. "That's *woman's work*," Mr. Taylor said.

Lexi was startled. That was a phrase she never heard in her own house.

"I don't have time to fool with it," he continued. "If she wants that thing fixed, she's going to have to do it herself."

Lexi thought she saw Mrs. Taylor's lips pucker in disapproval. Brock flushed at being corrected.

"Don't pay any attention to him, Lexi." Mrs. Taylor looked up from her work. "He's got some very antiquated ideas about the division of labor in this world. Brock, I hope you'll be more enlightened than your father."

"Aw, Mom," Brock growled, embarrassed.

"I've had a difficult time convincing Brock and his father that cooking and washing dishes aren't solely the domain of women. I'm not sure they'll *ever* believe that laundry and child care can also be done by the male species."

The dull ache in Lexi's head intensified, caused in part by a severe case of confusion. She *liked* Brock, she really did. He was nice to her, generous, kind, and pleasant. He was also incredibly good-looking. Unfortunately when she was with him she felt as though she were wearing a pair of shoes that didn't quite fit. His background, ideas, and attitudes were very different from hers. She felt a twinge of misery and guilt.

Lexi's father often said that people didn't appreciate what they had until they'd lost it. Perhaps she hadn't appreciated Todd enough until he was gone.

"Can I help you with that?" Lexi offered as Mrs. Taylor worked on the chandelier. "I'm good with my hands."

The older woman looked up with genuine gratitude in her eyes. "Thank you. I've been at this for hours. Some help would be wonderful."

Brock glanced warily at his father before sitting down next to Lexi. "I'll help too . . . just to keep you company." He relaxed when his father didn't comment.

In less than an hour they had the light fixture repaired.

"Lexi, you're a doll," Mrs. Taylor said. "I can't tell you how much I appreciate your help. Sometimes I get tired of these two macho men I have."

"Mom!"

Mrs. Taylor smiled and rubbed her son's back. "You've been listening to your dad all your life, Brock. I know, I understand."

As she watched mother and son exchange a glance, Lexi realized that it probably wasn't easy for Brock either, being torn between his mother's attitudes and those of his father.

She was still thinking about the odd chemistry at the Taylor house as Brock drove her home.

When Brock turned into the Leightons' driveway, he turned off the car lights.

Occupied with her own thoughts, Lexi was startled when she felt his arm go around her shoulders and his warm breath against her temple. Lexi turned her head just as Brock's kiss landed on her cheek.

"Quit squirming, Lexi." A note of impatience tinged his voice. At that moment, the garage door opened and light flooded into the front seat of Brock's car.

Brock muttered something unintelligible and likely unpleasant when Ben greeted them. "Hi, Lexi. I just walked Wiggles."

"Where are your manners, Ben? What do you say to Brock?"

"Hi, Brock," Ben said with little enthusiasm in his voice. More than once he'd expressed his dismay at Todd's absence from their household. Ben clearly blamed Brock for the change.

"Gotta go," Brock announced once it was clear that Ben was not going to leave them alone.

Ben and Lexi stood on the front step and waved as he drove away.

"What are you doing up so late, little guy? Why don't you go to bed? I'll take care of Wiggles for a while."

Ben nodded sleepily and trudged toward the stairs as Lexi picked up the puppy and walked into the living room.

The room was dark with shadows and shapes reflected in the light of a streetlamp. Lexi sat down on the floor, her back propped against the couch. She held Wiggles tightly to her chest.

"Oh, puppy, what am I going to do?" The little warm body squirmed against her. She could feel him gently licking the hollow spot at the base of her neck. There was something very comforting about a puppy. They asked no questions and made no demands.

"I really like Brock," she explained to the pup. Wiggles's breathing slowed as he relaxed against her chest. "He's handsome, charming, and fun, but there are things about him that just don't make me feel comfortable."

She thought about the episode with the waitress and the embarrassing fiasco at the fairgrounds. She recalled the times that Brock seemed to ignore people who didn't interest him—and the way he managed to charm anyone who did. Then tonight with the way his father had talked about "woman's work," and the way Brock's mother seemed to accept it.

"There's nothing really big and awful about him, Wiggles. I think he'd be a very nice boyfriend for someone. I'm just not sure that 'someone' is me."

Lexi scratched the sleepy puppy behind the ear. "It's good to have someone who will listen to me. At least I can be sure you won't repeat anything I say." Gently, Lexi carried Wiggles to his kennel. The puppy snuffled and sighed in his bed, gave two small thumps of his tail, and was asleep.

Lexi wished *she* could sleep so easily and so

soundly. She already knew that tonight would be a sleepless one. She closed her bedroom door and flung herself across her bed, feeling confused and very much alone.

Chapter Eleven

"Watch out!" Jennifer blurted as Lexi walked into the school.

"What for?" Everything seemed business-as-usual in the hallways.

"Binky is having a crisis."

"Now what?"

"You won't believe it," Jennifer grumbled as she fell into step beside Lexi. She's been reading her horoscope this morning."

"I was hoping she'd lose interest."

"That's not likely. You know Binky."

"What's the problem today?"

"She's worried about having had to come to school. She never goes out unless her horoscope recommends it."

"It's even *worse* when Binky's horoscope says it's a *good* day for socializing," Lexi pointed out. "Then she insists we all join her at whatever she's supposed to be doing. I've tried to convince her how stupid this is, but she simply won't listen."

"We're all tired of it, Lexi. I've come to the conclusion that Binky is addicted to the horoscope column in the newspaper. She won't make a move until she's consulted it."

At that moment Binky appeared, looking agitated. "I shouldn't even be here today!"

"Good morning to you too," Lexi responded.

"*Good* morning? How can you say that? Lexi, have you read your horoscope today?"

"No, and I don't plan to. I can get through the day without it just fine, thank you."

"I don't understand why you people are so careless with your lives! My horoscope said that I am going to have an absolutely awful day and that I shouldn't leave home. I can't believe my mother made me go to school."

"What *was* the woman thinking of?"

Binky missed the sarcasm in Jennifer's voice. "I don't know! How could she be so careless with her own children? I've tried to tell her how important this is. But will she listen to me? No.

"What if I get hit by a car or fail my English test? What if the supporting beams in the gymnasium give way and the ceiling comes tumbling down. . . ."

"I want to read that horoscope of yours, Binky," Lexi joked. "It must be a very dramatic prediction for today."

"I can't listen to this anymore," Jennifer announced abruptly. "I have to leave or I'm going to puke."

As she stomped off, Binky stared after her, puzzled. "What's wrong with her today? She's not under my sign. She *can't* be having as awful a day as I'm having!"

Everyone was growing tired of Binky's dependence on horoscopes. Lexi was at a loss as to how to convince her that they were nonsense.

"Binky, listen to yourself. You sound ridiculous."

"I know you refuse to take this seriously, but it makes a lot of sense. I've been doing some reading. . . ."

As the first class bell rang Binky made a small sound of dismay. "See? It's starting already. I'm going to be late for class. Save me a place at lunch, Lexi. With my luck today, there'll be nowhere in the cafeteria for me to sit. You'd better take a carton of chocolate milk for me too. By the time I get through the line, it will already be gone."

Binky dashed off, one shoelace untied, her blouse falling untucked from her jeans, her hair a mess—a whirlwind of a girl looking for disaster around every corner.

Binky's lunch tray landed on the table with a bang. "I can't believe it," she announced. "I've got homework."

"What's so unusual about that?" Anna Maria asked. "Isn't a teacher's job to torment us?"

"But tonight of all nights!"

"What's going on tonight?"

"My horoscope says I should take a night off because my mental capacity won't be up to my usual high standards. I'll probably do all my homework and get an *F* in every class tomorrow."

"When are you going to give up on this stupid horoscope stuff?" Angela asked.

"Stupid stuff? I've finally found something that puts order and reason into my life and you call it stupid?"

"It may be putting order and reason in *your* life, Binky, but it's making chaos of ours," Jennifer said grumpily. "It's driving us all nuts."

"I thought you guys were my friends." Tears filled Binky's eyes and one leaked forlornly down her cheek. "I thought you'd be *happy* for me."

"We *are* happy for you when something good happens. We just don't think this horoscope thing is good." Lexi put her hand on Jennifer's forearm to keep her from saying more.

"You just don't understand. My life is so much better now that I have a plan for each day. You should all be happy for me. Instead you're being mean." Binky looked terribly hurt. Her face was pinched and tight and her lower lip wobbled pitifully.

"I don't see why everyone is irritated with me." Binky shoved her tray away and stood up. "Of course, my horoscope *did* say that this was going to be an awful day." Binky walked away, her head held high, unbowed by the criticism of her beloved horoscopes.

"Now we've done it," Lexi groaned. "We've really hurt her feelings."

"She's been asking for it," Jennifer pointed out. "You know perfectly well that she'll make us crazy with that garbage."

"I'm worried about her." Angela frowned. "I talked to Egg. He's concerned too. This horoscope business is changing her. She's become dependent upon it to plan her life. Egg said their parents even punished Binky for refusing to go out with them. She'd told them that her horoscope recommended that she stay home that day and she simply wouldn't go."

"Binky's done a lot of crazy things, but until the

horoscope mess, she's never disobeyed her parents."

Until Jennifer said that, Lexi had been only partially paying attention to the conversation, her mind focused more on her own problems. "Binky's in trouble with her parents over this?"

"Egg says this horoscope thing has caused a lot of turmoil in their family," Angela informed them. "Mrs. McNaughton is upset by Binky's behavior. Binky doesn't want to make a move unless she consults her horoscope first."

"It's odd that Egg never said anything about it to me," Lexi murmured.

Jennifer gave her a pitying stare. "He probably did and you just didn't hear him."

"Why do you say that?"

"You haven't heard much of what any of us have said lately. Don't you realize that?"

Lexi digested her friends' words slowly. She'd been so wrapped up in her own problems that she hadn't even noticed just how troubled her friends had become.

"Have I been that bad?"

"Worse," Jennifer said bluntly. "It's like you're not even with us half the time. We talk to you and you don't answer. Binky's been wrecking things for us lately, Lexi, but so have you."

"Wrecking things? What do you mean?"

"Do you know where the guys are today?" Jennifer asked.

"No."

"They're ignoring us, that's where. Todd's been trying to give you some space; where Todd goes, Egg goes. Our group is falling apart, Lexi, and you haven't even noticed!"

Lexi looked at Jennifer's agitated face, then at Peggy's solemn one. Anna Marie and Angela looked equally somber.

"I'm so sorry," Lexi said softly. "I didn't realize . . . I just didn't *realize*, I'd been thinking about myself and my problems. I didn't even *see* what's been going on around me. I haven't been a very good friend to any of you lately, especially not to Binky."

"You don't have to be so hard on yourself," Peggy said.

"Yes I do. I know perfectly well that Binky's crazy ideas about horoscopes are hurting, not helping her. Binky and I have always been able to talk about our problems, and now when she really needs me, I haven't been there for her."

"It's not too late yet," Jennifer pointed out. "She *still* needs you."

"I'm going to talk to Binky right after school today. Sometimes she gets so involved in things that she loses perspective, that's all."

"It happens to the best of us," Jennifer said pointedly.

"I can always count on you to remind me when I goof up, can't I, Jennifer?"

"It's a dirty job, but somebody's got to do it. Good luck talking to Binky. It's not going to be easy."

On her way to her locker that afternoon, Lexi saw Brock wave to her but Lexi just quickened her steps. Todd was a few steps behind Brock. Lexi refused to look at him as well. Those boys had taken up far too much of her time lately. *Binky* was at the top of her priority list now.

"Wait!" Lexi caught Binky as she was about to leave the school building. "Can I walk home with you?"

Binky looked surprised. "I thought you'd be with Brock."

"Brock who?"

Binky smiled. "That's more like it. You've been off in a world of your own for so long, I thought you'd forgotten about the rest of us."

"Sorry about that. I had a lapse."

"I've missed you, Lexi," Binky said quietly.

Wasn't that just what Ben had said? Had she been that oblivious to her friends?

"I'm sorry I haven't been around for you. It's been a confusing time . . . Todd . . . Brock . . . you know. But I don't want to talk about that right now. I want to talk about you."

"What about me?"

"Let's start with that episode in the lunch room today."

"Oh, *that*," Binky blushed. "I was just a little emotional, that's all. I get shook up when I have a bad horoscope day."

"That's exactly what I want to talk about. You're putting much too much faith in those horoscopes."

"What's wrong with that?"

"I went to the library during study hall and did some research."

"Really? You did that for me?"

"I learned a lot too. I never realized how *many* astrologers there are in our country—thousands and thousands! Plus, two thousand or more newspapers carry daily horoscopes." Lexi glanced at Binky to see if her friend understood what she was getting at. "There's a lot of money to be earned from horoscopes."

"Money?" Binky looked blank. "Why?"

"Because once you read your horoscope for the day, you don't want to use it again, do you? You have to have a new one every morning. That's a great money-making opportunity for someone claiming to be an astrologer who wants to sell their horoscopes."

"Are you trying to tell me that people are only in this for the money?" Binky narrowed her eyes suspiciously. "I should have expected this from you."

"Did you know that the earliest form of astrology was connected to star worship?" Lexi quickly attempted to divert Binky.

"Worship? Like in church?"

"People worshiped the stars because they thought they were gods and had power over man."

Binky looked interested and a little unsure as Lexi continued.

"A man named Ptolemy is given the credit for today's zodiac and method of doing horoscopes based on the positions of the sun, moon, and planets at the time of a person's birth."

Binky wrinkled her nose. "I didn't know about all of this. It's very confusing."

"The books I read said the same thing. In fact, my research said that astrologers often draw up conflicting horoscopes for the same people. Every astrologer wants their prediction to be the right one so they run down the predictions of others.

"If horoscopes are correct, then all twins should experience the very same personalities, life events—even deaths. After all, they're born under the same sign!"

"Are you making this up?" Binky asked suspiciously. "To confuse me?"

"No. I'm just telling you what I read. All the books I found said that serious astrologers don't accept the astrological columns in newspapers because the readings are based on the position of the sun at the time of birth."

"I didn't know any of that stuff," Binky blurted.

"I didn't know much either," Lexi admitted. "I feel very uncomfortable about horoscopes. It seems . . . all wrong."

Lexi realized that they were walking by her church. Pastor Lake's car was in the parking lot. "Let's ask Pastor Lake what he thinks about horoscopes."

"Do you think he'd have an opinion?" Binky looked surprised.

"I'm sure he would. You're letting these horoscopes guide your life, Binky. God is the only One who should be doing that."

Binky glanced at her watch. "Okay, I've got time. Let's go inside."

Pastor Lake was in his office. He was wearing jeans and his shirt-sleeves were rolled to his elbows. He looked very young and unpastor-like. That made it easy for Binky and Lexi to approach him with their questions.

"So you want to know about astrology." He tilted backward in his chair and crossed his arms over his chest. "You girls don't ask easy questions, do you?"

"Does it say anything about astrology in the Bible?" Binky wondered eagerly.

"Oh yes, but not with much kindness. The prophet Jeremiah predicted God's judgment on Israel because it was involved in star worship. Jeremiah nineteen verse thirteen says, '*And I will defile all the homes in Jerusalem, including the palace of the Kings of Judah—wherever incense has been burned upon the roofs to your stargods, and libations poured out to them.*' "

"Stargods, huh? That sounds awful!"

"Later the church viewed astrology as satanic fortune-telling. Once people began to understand the stars scientifically, astronomy took some of the power from astrology. Still, it seems when people are feeling empty and looking for meaning in their lives, they'll turn to anything that offers them hope, order, or sense in their lives. That's why astrology thrives during times of faithlessness in religion. Unfortunately we're seeing more believers in astrology now than we have for a long time."

"But it *works*!" Binky protested.

"If it really does work as well as you say, then why haven't the astrologers who have been practicing throughout history all become millionaires?"

"Huh?" Binky frowned darkly. "What do you mean?"

"Using their own predictions they should have known when to buy and sell stock or bet on horse races. They should have known when to avoid investing and when to plunge in full steam ahead. Correct?"

"I suppose, but . . ."

"Binky, if astrologers have such an inside track on the world, then why aren't their lives perfect?

And why haven't we heard about these perfect lives?"

"But I've read books that give examples of how astrologers foretold the future . . ."

"Did they mention the times that their predictions were wrong?"

"No, of course not."

"I wouldn't admit to my mistakes either—especially if those admissions would destroy my business. Binky, the astrological predictions you're reading in the newspaper are so vague that you and I could write them and be correct most of the time!"

Pastor Lake reached for his Bible. "Let's take a look at Isaiah forty-seven: *"You have advisors by the ton—your astrologers and stargazers, who try to tell you what the future holds. But they are as useless as dried grass burning in the fire. They cannot even deliver themselves! You'll get no help from them at all. Theirs is no fire to sit beside to make you warm!"*

"The Bible says that?" Binky looked horrified. "I didn't think there was any *harm* in believing in this. . . ."

"No harm?" Lexi blurted. "You're already a prisoner to your horoscope! You won't go out if it tells you to stay in. If it says you'll have a horrible day, you make sure that you do."

"Some people allow astrologers to control their decision to marry, to have children, to travel. It can be an all-consuming belief. Quit waiting for an astrologer to tell you how to live your life—those decisions should be up to you and to God!"

"About God . . ." Binky began. "Does this mean that astrology isn't Christian?"

"That's exactly what it means. Astrologers are

what the Bible called 'false prophets' because their predictions do not all come true."

"Shouldn't everyone get to make a little mistake once in a while?" Binky asked.

"Not if they claim to be prophets. It says in Deuteronomy that if the thing someone prophesies doesn't happen, then it isn't the Lord who has given him the message; he has made it up himself.

"God is perfect, Binky, and He's made us to be like Him. He has made us to be free to serve Him, not to be subjected to the tyranny of astrologers or anyone else. Astrology doesn't belong in the life of a Christian."

"Boy, do I feel dumb." Binky's expression was downcast. "I really blew it this time. I actually believed in all that star stuff!"

"Stars are good, Binky. After all, they are part of God's creation! But they can't tell us how to live our lives. Only God can do that."

Chapter Twelve

"Lexi," Mrs. Leighton called. "Binky's on the phone."

"I'll take it upstairs." Lexi picked up the telephone in her mother's room and flopped down on her parents' bed.

"Hi, Bink. What's up?"

"I've been thinking."

"Pretty dangerous activity," Lexi joked.

"I've felt weird ever since we had that conversation with Pastor Lake and he suggested that I not read my horoscope anymore."

"How does it feel?"

"Kind of empty right now," Binky admitted. "But I realize this is the right thing to do." She hesitated before adding, "There's something else I need to do as well. It's Brock. . . ."

"What about him?" He'd phoned several times today but Lexi hadn't taken his calls.

"I just wanted you to know that I think that Brock is really nice . . . to you at least."

"*Just* to me, not to anyone else?"

"Oh, he's nice to some people, but not to everyone. He's always nice to the people he thinks are important. I doubt he knows Egg and I exist."

"Don't be silly."

"I mean it. We're not important to him socially, so he doesn't even know we're around."

"Aren't you being a little hard on him?" But in her heart Lexi knew that Binky had put her finger on something that had been bothering her as well. Brock was "status conscious." He was nice to certain people and ignored all the others.

Lexi had assumed that he hadn't been intentionally unkind, but Brock often acted like some people were beneath him and not worthy of his courtesy.

"I don't want to say anything bad about Brock," Binky continued, "because there are a lot of great things about him. He's smart, funny, and handsome. Plus, he's really nice to you and that's great. Though he's nice *to* you, Lexi, I don't think he's nice *for* you."

"Why do you say that?"

"It's hard to explain." Binky sounded both nervous and puzzled. "I think his value system is different than yours."

"Value system?"

"The things he thinks are important. *Who* he thinks is important. Lexi, you're not a snob. You're the *nicest*, most generous, compassionate, and accepting person I've ever met. That's why I like you so much. But Brock's not like you. He's only interested in perfect people."

"Well, I'm hardly perfect."

"You're pretty, smart, and fun to be with. Girls and guys both like you. Until Brock came along, you had a great-looking boyfriend—one of the most popular guys in school. Now you're one of Brock's conquests."

"Conquests? You make me sound like a hunting trophy! Besides, I can't believe that Brock would . . ."

"He was rude to Egg," Binky said. "Egg wasn't going to tell me, but he moped around the house until I made him talk."

"What did Brock do?" Lexi had a sinking feeling in the pit of her stomach.

"For starters, he called Egg a geek. Frankly, my brother *is* a geek. You and I know that, but he's our kind of geek and we love him for it. He's always been sensitive about how tall and skinny he is and how big his Adam's apple is. My parents tell him that he's going to catch up with himself one day and look just fine. But it doesn't help to have someone like Brock telling him he's goofy. *I'm* the only who can call my brother goofy!"

"I didn't know . . ."

"What's more," Binky continued, determined, "Brock told Todd that his *ex*-girlfriend was 'a real hot babe.' I think that's rude, don't you? He was actually boasting that he'd stolen away Todd's girlfriend!"

"I can't be stolen. I'm not property," Lexi protested.

"You'd better tell Brock that."

Lexi didn't like what she was hearing. She knew others thought Brock was both snobbish and possessive. If she'd dared to admit it from the times she'd visited his home, she too had had the idea that Brock's father's attitude was much the same toward his mother.

She *liked* Brock. She genuinely did, but they were not a good fit together. Her faith was important, as were the people around her—popular and beautiful or not—and Brock didn't fully share those values.

"I have noticed certain things about Brock," Lexi said reluctantly, "but I never realized. . . . Maybe I've ignored things that I shouldn't have just because Brock is so nice to me.

"I'm sorry Brock hurt you and Egg," Lexi continued. "But I do appreciate your honesty."

"And I appreciated yours about the horoscopes. It's a bummer to hear you're on the wrong track, isn't it?"

Lexi winced at Binky's meaning . . . Brock. They talked a few more moments before hanging up. Then Lexi lay on her parents' bed and stared at the ceiling.

With dismay, she realized that her conversation with Binky had changed everything.

Lexi picked up the phone and dialed Jennifer's number. "I have a question for you."

"Okay."

"What's the deal between Todd and Molly?"

Jennifer was silent for a long moment. "Do you really want to know?"

"I think I'd *better* know!"

"A lot of people assume they're going out. Molly has been telling people that Todd's her new boyfriend. I don't know if Todd agrees with her or not. What happened, Lexi? How did you and Todd drift so far apart?"

"I don't know. It just happened. I didn't mean for things to work out this way. When Brock came to town, he drove a wedge between us that kept getting wider and wider, without Todd and me ever having a fight or even a decent conversation about what was going wrong. Now what am I going to do?"

"It's too bad Binky's thrown away her horoscope books. You could have consulted them." Jennifer's attempt at a joke failed miserably.

Lexi struggled to say goodbye before she burst into tears.

Mrs. Leighton found her sometime later, curled up on the bed.

"What's wrong, honey? Are you sick?"

"Oh, Mom!" Lexi launched herself into her mother's arms. "I've ruined everything."

"Everything?" Her mother smoothed the hair out of Lexi's eyes. "I don't believe you've ruined *everything*."

"I've lost Todd and it's my own doing. I got caught up with Brock because he's so handsome and charming, and I refused to look at the person that he is. Brock's not like me, Mom."

"And Todd is?"

"At least we think the same things are important. Brock and I never talked about whether or not he believes in God. That's important in my life, Mom, and I didn't even bring up the subject with him because I was afraid of his answer! I wanted to be with a handsome new guy no matter what it cost."

"You're not the first girl guilty of that. Nor will you be the last."

"But I've made a mess of things! Brock wants to be with me now and Todd's found someone else."

Mrs. Leighton cradled Lexi in her arms and

rocked back and forth, much as she'd done when Lexi was a small child. "When you were little, and you fell down and scraped your knee, I could wash it, put a bandage on it, kiss it, and make it feel better. Even when you were older, I could coax or cuddle you out of your sadness. I can't anymore. You're on the verge of adulthood. Your problems are bigger now and solutions harder. When you become an adult, you have to start looking for your own answers."

"Then being an adult isn't much fun."

Mrs. Leighton laughed softly. "No, not always. It has drawbacks. It also has its rewards."

"Will anything good come out of this?" Lexi wondered morosely.

"Even bad experiences can be turned into better ones, if you learn from them."

"All I've learned is that I'm an idiot."

"You've learned more than that. You've learned not to be charmed by looks alone, haven't you?"

"That's true."

Mrs. Leighton gently wiped a tear away from Lexi's cheek with her thumb. "You'll be much wiser next time."

"This is too hard," Lexi protested.

"Lots of things in life are hard," Mrs. Leighton said pragmatically. "That's how people grow up, by surviving a few hard lessons." She looked at her daughter and smiled. "This doesn't feel like it's helping very much, does it, Lexi?"

"No. I wish you could fix things just like when I was little."

"One thing has always stayed the same, Lexi. You still have your family. No matter what, we'll always be here for you and we'll always love you."

"Even when I make stupid decisions?"

"Especially then."

At that moment Ben and Wiggles burst into the bedroom. "Are you sick, Lexi?" Ben challenged.

"No, Ben. Just down in the dumps."

He scrambled onto the bed, Wiggles in tow. "Me and Wiggles will take you out of the dumps."

Obligingly, Wiggles licked Lexi's face.

All the love, concern, and affection from her family felt wonderful. But it was not enough to keep Lexi from falling asleep that night crying into her pillow.

Chapter Thirteen

"Lexi, can you hear me? Wake up." The panic in her mother's voice made Lexi's eyes fly open.

"What's wrong?"

"You have to help me find Ben."

Lexi rolled over to look at her alarm clock. "It's eight o'clock on a Saturday morning. Isn't he sleeping?"

"He got up early to take the dog out. I was still half asleep, so I told him to put Wiggles in the backyard. I can't believe it, but I fell back asleep again. I just woke up and neither Ben nor the puppy is anywhere nearby. Your dad has taken the car to go look for them. I want you to get dressed and help me." Mrs. Leighton ran her fingers through her hair and Lexi could see that her hand was trembling.

Lexi jumped out of bed and pulled on a pair of jeans and a sweatshirt. She slid her feet into a pair of loafers and was downstairs almost as quickly as her mother.

"We're going to need more help, Lexi. I have no idea where those two have gone."

"I'll call a couple of my friends. Don't worry, we'll find them." Lexi dialed Jennifer's number.

"Jen, you have to come quick. Ben and Wiggles are missing."

"Not again!" Lexi heard the immediate fear in Jennifer's voice.

This had happened before, shortly after the Leightons had moved to Cedar River. That time, Benjamin had been hit by a car. . . .

"Call some others, Jen. You've got to help us find him."

Lexi dialed again.

"Hullo." The voice on the other end of the line was thick with sleep.

"Brock, I'm sorry to wake you."

"Who is this?"

"It's Lexi."

"What are you doing up so early?"

"I need some help. . . ."

"I'll help you later. Call me back at a civilized hour."

"But Brock . . ."

"It's a Saturday morning, Lexi. I'm sure it can wait. Give me a break. Call at noon."

Lexi stared at the telephone as the dial tone buzzed in her ear. He'd hung up on her!

I'm sure it can wait.

Is that what he thought? That friendships could be put on hold? That relationships could be turned off and on like water faucets or electric lights?

"Well, if that's what you think, Brock Taylor, you're wrong!"

She would *never* have done to any of her friends what Brock had just done to her! Never, ever. It was as though blinders had been lifted from her eyes and she could see things clearly for the first time.

Brock was totally selfish! He was also charming, handsome, and intelligent—almost everything a girl could want in a boy—except thoughtful, considerate, and accepting of others. And those were qualities Lexi knew she couldn't live without.

Wiping away a tear with the back of her hand, she hurried into the yard. She was surprised to see that her friends had already gathered there—Jennifer, Egg, Binky, Peggy, and . . . could it be? Todd.

They all looked as though they'd just rolled out of bed. Egg was wearing his pajama top stuffed carelessly into a pair of jeans. He was also wearing bedroom slippers.

In spite of the fear and emotion rocketing within her, Lexi had to smile. *These* were the people that cared about her most. They were the ones who deserved her loyalty and affection.

"Everyone, break into pairs. I have already circled these blocks." Mrs. Leighton was taking charge. "Egg and Binky, you go east. Peggy and Jennifer, south. Todd and Lexi, north. I'll go west. Wiggles doesn't respond to his name yet. You'd better just call for Ben."

"We'll take my car," Todd said to Lexi as the others began to fan out on their mission. "We can cover more territory that way. You can hang out the window and holler Ben's name."

Lexi nodded, grateful for the brisk, businesslike way Todd was handling himself. If he hadn't, she feared she might burst into tears.

"This is weird," Todd said as they drove. "It reminds me of . . . never mind."

"Of the night Ben was hit by Jerry's car?"

"I'm sorry. I shouldn't have brought it up."

"I'd thought of it already. Ben's older now—and hopefully wiser. Besides, he's very protective of that puppy. I don't think he'd do anything careless or foolish with Wiggles."

"You're being very brave, Lexi." She could hear the admiration in Todd's voice.

"No, I'm not. I'm terrified. We both know how vulnerable Ben is."

As they drove, both Todd and Lexi scanned the streets for signs of a dark-haired boy and a small dog.

"Do you think the others have had any luck?" Lexi asked.

"I don't know. I don't think Ben could have gotten much farther than this. Maybe we should turn back." Todd glanced at Lexi. "I've been praying for him, Lexi."

Lexi smiled, her grin watery. "I know. I have too."

What other guy would do that for her and her little brother? she wondered. There weren't many. Certainly not Brock.

She was thrown off balance as Todd pulled the wheel of the car sharply to the right. "What's wrong?"

"I thought of someplace we need to look." His voice had an odd sound. "There's a drainage ditch a block or two from here. . . ."

"Oh, Ben wouldn't go near that. It's full of water right now and . . . You don't think . . ." The icy hand of fear clutched at Lexi's heart. Ben was no swimmer. He was a little boy out for a walk with his puppy. If the puppy got thirsty and Ben thought the pup needed a drink . . .

The drainage ditch looked deceptively peaceful. Todd parked the car and they both jumped out. There was no activity nearby. "We'll just walk up and down this area," Todd suggested. "He's probably not here, but just in case . . ." His voice trailed away as Wiggles came bounding toward them with his big blue leash dragging behind him. The puppy yapped and squirmed at the sight of Lexi. When Lexi kneeled down to pick him up, Wiggles bathed her face with his tongue in a grateful show of affection.

"Where's Ben, Wiggles? Where's Ben?"

She looked up at Todd, her face pale. "Ben would never leave the dog intentionally. Never."

Todd broke into a run toward the ditch. Lexi tucked Wiggles under one arm and followed him.

"Todd, where are you?" She lost sight of him as he bolted over a rise.

"Over here, Lexi. Come quick."

Lexi raced toward the sound of Todd's voice. She found him on the far side of a rolling incline, crouched next to her brother.

"Benjamin!" Lexi shouted so loud Ben jumped. "Are you all right?"

"No, I'm not." The little boy had been crying.

"He twisted his ankle." Todd examined the injured foot, which had already started to swell.

"My toes gots stucked in there." Ben pointed to a small gopher hole. "You found help for me, didn't you, Wiggles?"

Lexi put the puppy on the ground and he ran directly into Ben's arms.

"Wiggles stayed with me. I was crying and he licked my face and he made me feel better."

"That's a good dog," Lexi whispered, overwhelmed with emotion.

"I woulda been scared if I was alone, but I knew Wiggles would take care of me."

Lexi glanced at the small puppy who'd been entrusted with so much responsibility. He was curled into Ben's lap.

"Why was Wiggles running along the ditch when we found him?"

"Because I sent him for help," Ben explained. "He didn't wanna go. I had to yell and clap my hands and say, 'Go find Lexi.' And you found her, didn't you?" Ben kissed the top of the dog's head. "You're my best friend in the whole world."

She couldn't stop her emotions any longer. Tears welled in Lexi's eyes.

Todd glanced up from where he was crouched. "Cry all you want, Lexi. I feel like it too." Then he picked Ben up, puppy and all. "You're getting heavy, Ben. What have you been eating?"

"Bricks." Ben giggled. "But Wiggles is the fat one."

"*Somebody* is heavy." Todd carried his burden to the car and placed Ben in the passenger seat. Then he turned to Lexi and, without a word, put his arms around her. As she cried, Todd held her close. He stroked her hair and crooned gentle, comforting words into her ear.

"We'd better tell your mom we found him." Todd finally pointed out, "She must be frantic by now."

They found Dr. and Mrs. Leighton only two blocks away. Ever-practical Dr. Leighton suggested that Ben be taken home and given a bath and some ice for his ankle.

"I'll drop them off and then find your friends to tell them we've located our missing boy," her dad continued. "You have some wonderful friends, Lexi. You're a lucky young woman."

After Dr. and Mrs. Leighton left, Todd and Lexi hesitated, neither quite ready to see the others. Todd leaned against his car and let the morning sunlight warm his face.

"I think we could learn something from those two," he finally commented.

"Ben and Wiggles, you mean?"

Todd nodded and bit the corner of his lip thoughtfully. "It appears they know more about loyalty and friendship than we do. I have to apologize to you, Lexi."

"You? Apologize to me? Why?"

"For being jealous of Brock. And for pushing you into a corner. I've thought about it a lot. Maybe if I'd been a little cooler about the whole thing, none of this would have happened. You have a right to have other friends. I shouldn't have assumed you were mine, like a piece of property. I'm sorry."

"Todd, you don't have to apologize. You didn't do anything wrong."

"Didn't I? Once I saw you and Brock growing closer, I took out Molly to make you angry. It was a dirty trick. I never really liked her but I led her on to make you jealous."

"Oh, Todd . . ."

"Molly is really a great person, Lexi, but she's not my type. I apologized to her yesterday for leading her on."

"You did that?" Lexi was stunned.

"I'm not sure she's going to accept my apology.

She was furious with me, but I couldn't continue the way I was going. I didn't feel comfortable using another person to hurt you. I've learned my lesson. Even if you never come back to me, Lexi, I'd never hurt someone else to attempt to make it happen. That's a rotten trick to play and I've hated myself for it."

"Mom says that sometimes lessons are the only good thing that come out of bad situations."

"You've talked to your mother about us?"

"I've been miserable too, Todd. I've hated what happened between us. I suppose I was curious to know what it was like to date another guy. Brock was charming and friendly and flattering. I fell for it, but I learned a lesson from him too."

"What was that?" Todd's expression was wary.

"I learned that the better I got to know Brock, the more I missed you. Our friendship is more important than all the dating relationships in the world, Todd. I'm sorry too for being such a lousy friend to you."

"That's what I missed too—our friendship. Knowing I could call you, and that you'd always listen."

"Is there any chance we can still be best friends after what I've done to you?"

"A really good chance." Todd put his arm around Lexi and gave her a hug. "I'm glad Ben has a friend like Wiggles," he said, "and I'm glad I have a friend like you."

"Let's go find Jennifer and the others," Lexi suggested. "Now that Binky is out of her horoscope phase and you and I have made up, they're all going to be relieved."

"Right. And for once I have a prediction of my own. I'm going to have a very happy afternoon."

"That's one prediction I'd have to agree with."

Lexi tucked her hand in Todd's and they went to find their friends.

Something is terribly wrong with Lexi's mom. Can Lexi handle her mother's illness? Find out in Cedar River Daydreams #23.

A Note From Judy

I'm glad you're reading *Cedar River Daydreams*! I hope I've given you something to think about as well as a story to entertain you. If you feel you have any of the problems that Lexi and her friends experience, I encourage you to talk with your parents, a pastor, or a trusted adult friend. There are many people who care about you!

I love to hear from my readers, so if you'd like to receive my newsletter and a bookmark, please send a self-addressed, stamped envelope to:

Judy Baer
Bethany House Publishers
11300 Hampshire Avenue South
Minneapolis, MN 55438

Be sure to watch for my newest *Dear Judy . . .* books at your local bookstore. These books are full of questions that you, my readers, have asked in your letters, along with my response. Just about every topic is covered—from dating and romance to friendships and parents. Hope to hear from you soon!

Dear Judy, What's It Like at Your House?
Dear Judy, Did You Ever Like a Boy (Who Didn't Like You?)

Live! From Brentwood High

1 ▪ Risky Assignment
2 ▪ Price of Silence
3 ▪ Double Danger
4 ▪ Sarah's Dilemma
5 ▪ Undercover Artists

Other Books by Judy Baer

- Paige
- Adrienne
- Dear Judy, What's It Like at Your House?
- Dear Judy, Did You Ever Like a Boy (who didn't like you?)

9602